Josh quickly skimmed the article in Laura's typewriter. Surprised, he looked up and said, "This is really good."

"You don't have to act so shocked. Why does that fact surprise you? You don't even know me!" Laura said fiercely.

He walked toward her and gazed into eyes that held anger and hurt. "I know everything I need to know about you. You're kind, gentle, and your eyes sparkle with fire. Your voice gets husky when you're tired, and you have the annoying habit of being right most of the time." His finger reached out and traced her lower lip. "You're intelligent and blessed with the talent to make our simple scavenger hunt seem like the adventure of a lifetime." His hand cupped her cheek and angled her face upward. "Your kisses are addictive and your body responds like molten fire to my every touch."

Laura's hungry gaze focused on Josh's lips. No man had ever said such things to her before.

"Your eyes are speaking to me, Laura, but I need to hear the words. Tell me what you want," Josh said.

Her voice trembled with desire. "I want you to kiss me."

A smile played at the corner of his mouth. "I thought you'd never ask. . . ."

WHAT ARE *LOVESWEPT* ROMANCES?

They are stories of true romance and touching emotion. We believe those two very important ingredients are constants in our highly sensual and very believable stories in the *LOVESWEPT* line. Our goal is to give you, the reader, stories of consistently high quality that may sometimes make you laugh, sometimes make you cry, but are always fresh and creative and contain many delightful surprises within their pages.

Most romance fans read an enormous number of books. Those they truly love, they keep. Others may be traded with friends and soon forgotten. We hope that each *LOVESWEPT* romance will be a treasure—a "keeper." We will always try to publish

LOVE STORIES YOU'LL NEVER FORGET
BY AUTHORS YOU'LL ALWAYS REMEMBER

The Editors

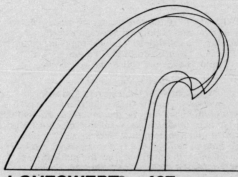

LOVESWEPT® • 467
Marcia Evanick
Guardian Spirit

BANTAM BOOKS
NEW YORK • TORONTO • LONDON • SYDNEY • AUCKLAND

GUARDIAN SPIRIT

A Bantam Book / April 1991

Bantam Books are published by Bantam Books, a
division of Bantam Doubleday Dell Publishing Group,
Inc. Its trademark, consisting of the words "Bantam
Books" and the portrayal of a rooster, is Registered in
U.S. Patent and Trademark Office and in other coun-
tries. Marca Registrada. Bantam Books, 666 Fifth Avenue, New York, New York 10103.

To my agent, Elaine Davie, who believes . . .

Thanks

Prologue

"I don't care whose turn it is. I don't want to go."

"Crazy Bear, you must go. She is calling you."

Crazy Bear stared down at the top of the mesa, at the proud face gazing heavenward, and grunted. *"Why can't One Paddle go?"*

"One Paddle would never do, he travels in circles. It's you she is calling."

"Her blood is thin. There's barely any Navaho left." Still, he felt his heart soften as he studied her sunburned face and dazed brown eyes.

"She's strong. She climbed halfway to heaven for you."

She stared upward, her chapped lips moving in the ancient chant. The heavens groaned as Crazy Bear stood and reached for his weapons. *"I always thought, when it was my turn to go, I'd find a strong young brave ready to go into battle."*

"The time for battle is past. We must learn to live in peace with the white man. Go, my brother, and help guide her through life."

A deep grunt escaped Crazy Bear's chest, then he stretched and dusted off his moccasins. He stood with his feet braced apart and arms flung wide to encompass the heavens. With a smile for his friend he said, *"It will be good to walk again the forgotten paths of our people."* He watched as the heavens darkened and lightning flew downward toward the maiden. In a final gesture of farewell he turned to his friend and a wolfish gleam sparked in his dark eyes. *"At least she's a fine-looking maiden."*

"Crazy Bear, remember the code of the Guardians. We have enough problems concerning our people. Don't add to them."

"Have I ever caused you problems?"

The heavens trembled and turned black. A thick cloud of smoke lingered where Crazy Bear had stood moments before.

A sad, worried voice drifted down. *"I hope you realize what you started, Laura Bryant."*

One

Ten years later . . .

Laura Ann Bryant held her breath as her battered Jeep coasted into the gas station, backfired twice, and died in front of the pump. She'd made it! Gingerly she opened the door and stepped out into a cloud of exhaust fumes still billowing from the back of the Jeep.

Josh Langley, sitting in his police cruiser on the far side of the station, heard the backfire and raised his head from the report he was filling out. A dilapidated Jeep towing an ancient horse trailer sat in front of the pumps. He grimaced when he saw a cloud of black smoke erupt from the tailpipe. Whoever was driving the Jeep deserved a ticket for polluting the air.

He set the clipboard down and unfastened his seat belt, then froze. The rusty door on the driver's side of the Jeep creaked open, and a petite foot wearing a sandal trimmed with colored beads appeared. It was followed by a bare, slim calf, a shapely knee, and a long, silky, tanned thigh. The foot was set gingerly on the steaming black asphalt, then a second leg joined the first. Josh's breath caught as his gaze traveled over snug denim shorts caressing a pert bottom, then skimmed a small waist and encountered a pair of perfect breasts. The vision was wearing a fluorescent orange tank top that molded the curves of her body.

Josh dragged air into his starved lungs and forced himself to look higher. At that same instant the vision turned her back and reached for the gas hose. Wavy brown hair was tied back into a haphazard ponytail by a piece of string. He glimpsed a large, generous mouth and huge sunglasses before she walked toward the front of the Jeep and popped the hood. Fascinated, he watched as she bent over the dented fender and dumped two quarts of oil into the engine. With a resounding thud she slammed the hood and patted the only clean spot on the vehicle. Then she quickly disengaged the gas hose, grabbed her purse, and walked into the station.

Before he could collect his scattered senses, she strolled back to the Jeep, got in, and started it up. The vehicle's thunderous backfire as she pulled onto the highway brought Josh out of his daze. The puff of smoke disappeared as he watched the rickety horse trailer sway down the road.

Unconcerned about her Jeep's noisy departure from the station, Laura glanced at the maps scattered among the potted cactuses next to her and laughed. She didn't need them any longer. Her cross-country adventure was over. She was home. A smile curved her lips. She liked the sound of that—home. Union Station, Pennsylvania, was now officially her home.

She drove down Main Street and marveled again at her feelings. It felt like home. Last month, when she had visited her childhood friend Kelli Sinclair, she'd walked this street until she knew it by heart. Everything was on Main Street. The bank, grocery store, pharmacy, and town hall. The town square, which boasted a gazebo and a war memorial, separated the flow of traffic. On one of her walks she had found the office of the town's local weekly newspaper, *The Union Station Review*. She'd stared at the help-wanted sign until she had gathered up her courage and opened the aged oak door. By that afternoon she was gainfully employed and talking to the one and only real estate agent in town.

After looking at five houses that were within her budget, the disgruntled agent had told her there was only one house left—the old Peterson place.

"The old Peterson place" turned out to be a decaying house with sagging porches and an overgrown yard. Laura wasn't positive of its style. In the shadow of three gigantic oaks, its dark gray paint peeling, its mansard roof, it reminded her of something Norman Bates would live in. The real estate agent reluctantly explained that the neighborhood children believed the house was haunted. Laura laughed and inspected the interior. Two hours later they had old man Peterson's only living relative on the phone, negotiating a lower price.

Laura turned the corner of Sixth Street and headed up the small hill toward home. The final papers had been sent the week before. She was now the proud owner of a haunted house. She chuckled as she pulled up into her drive. The ghost story had been worth several thousand dollars off the price of the house.

The Jeep shuddered to a halt at the back of the drive. With a flourish she threw open the driver's door and jumped out. Unlocking the kitchen door, she stepped over the threshold.

It was just as she remembered. Glass-front oak cabinets hung on walls covered in 1950-style wallpaper of coffee grinders, frying pans, and percolators. A chipped white porcelain sink contained an assortment of stains, and cobwebs hung from every corner of the ceiling.

She left the door open for fresh air and went exploring. Besides cobwebs, dust, and the occasional hanging light, the remaining downstairs rooms were empty. Using all her strength, she yanked open the front door, then peered through the screen. The yard had been cut, or, to be more accurate, scalped. Patches of dirt dotted the weed-choked grass. Someone had even run the lawn mower through the overgrown flower gardens. She glanced at the massive oak trees and wondered what they would look like cut back to a more manageable size.

Turning from the view, she tried the light switch. Lights! At least the electric company had turned on the electricity on schedule. Carrying candles around a presumably haunted house wasn't her idea of fun.

She hurried up the stairs, making a mental list of the chores to be done immediately. When the third step creaked under her weight, she stifled a scream. Laughing at her own foolishness, she continued up the steps. If she wasn't careful, she'd start to believe those childish stories. If there was one thing Laura Bryant didn't believe in, it was ghosts. Guardian spirits yes, but ghosts never.

"Go home, Kelli. Don't you have a business to run?"

"Gee, Laura, I only came to help."

Laura stared pointedly at Kelli's enlarged stomach. "The last I heard, Fairyland still needed a hostess." She smiled at her childhood friend and blessed the day, last year, when Logan Sinclair had called and demanded to know if she was the Laura Bryant who'd been in the same foster home as Kelli SanteFe nineteen years earlier. That early-morning call had renewed a friendship and earned the phone company a substantial profit. "It's ninety degrees outside," Laura added. "You look like you're smuggling watermelons, and your ankles are swollen. Go home and take a nap, or whatever else fat ladies do."

"I'm not fat," Kelli said with a huff. "I'm pregnant."

Laura chuckled. "I hadn't noticed." When a hurt look crossed her best friend's face, she said quickly, "I'm sorry, Kelli. Of course I noticed. It's the most wonderfully perfect belly I've ever seen."

"Logan thinks so too."

"Well, he should. He's the one who caused it. Now that you have checked up on me, go home. I'm fine, the refrigerator is working and full, and the water's not brown any longer."

"Are you sure?"

"Positive, so don't go eyeing those cleaning supplies piled in the corner. I've been on my own for ten years. I think I can handle knocking down cobwebs."

Kelli walked outside and smiled at Laura. "I'm going, see." She climbed into a minivan and rolled down the window. "Logan will be here by six to carry in what little furniture you've packed in that sorry excuse for a horse trailer."

"I'll accept his help this time, but remember, you both have a daughter at home, another child on the way, and his aunt and uncle to take care of. I also know how you love to mother anyone around. I don't need mothering, friend, you do. Now, go home and put those feet up."

"Gosh, I never realized you were so grouchy. Throwing defenseless pregnant ladies out of your home. You really should be ashamed of yourself."

"If you don't put this van into gear and get home, I'll tell Logan you tried to carry in the groceries."

"Don't you dare! You have no idea what he'd do.

He already has a cleaning woman coming in four days a week, two teenage boys handling the ground work at Fairyland, and I get to point to what I want done."

"I'm counting. One . . . two . . ." Laura laughed as the van backed out of the driveway and headed down the street.

"I'm telling you, Logan, we can manage."

"I'm sure we can, but you look half dead already." Logan flashed Laura a boyish smile. "Besides, Josh will be here any minute."

Laura glared at Kelli's handsome husband. The previous year he had spent a bundle locating a lost childhood friend for his wife's Christmas present. Within two weeks he had flown his entire family out to New Mexico for the reunion. He had lovingly watched their daughter while Kelli and Laura had spent days catching up. When they boarded the plane for their return flight, he had passed out tissues and the order that Laura would be visiting Pennsylvania come springtime. Even if he had to fly back to New Mexico to get her. Laura thought Kelli had found a terrific husband, but she was almost too used to doing everything for herself.

"How Kelli puts up with your high-handed attitude is beyond me," she muttered. "You didn't have to get your friend to help."

Logan walked around the back of the horse trailer, shaking his head. "How this thing made it across the country is beyond *me*. Frowning he kicked a bald tire on the trailer. "You have to meet Josh anyway. Mrs. Billington told Kelli your first assignment for the paper will be joining the scavenger hunt and reporting on it from a participant's point of view. Kelli already lined up Josh to be your partner."

"My partner?"

"You have to have a partner to enter."

Laura opened the passenger door on the Jeep and handed Logan a potted cactus. "Why did Mrs. Billington tell Kelli what my first assignment was?"

"One thing you'll learn about this town, there are no secrets. Everybody knows everybody else's business. Besides, Mrs. Billington asked Kelli about finding you a partner for the hunt."

Laura handed him another cactus and picked up two more. Preceding him into the house, she placed the plants on the floor near the living room windows. "When is this scavenger hunt?"

"This weekend."

Laura listened to the sound of a vehicle pulling into the driveway. "Sounds like your friend has arrived. Do you think I should warn him that I'm a sore loser?"

"No need. With Josh as your partner, you're bound to win."

"Has he won it before?"

"Nope. This is the first time he's entered."

"Oh, great, an amateur! What I need is someone with experience. I haven't been in a scavenger hunt since I was in Girl Scouts."

Logan chuckled as he headed out the kitchen door to greet his friend.

Josh parked the police cruiser behind Logan's van and stared at the sinister-looking house. Laura Bryant needed therapy, he decided. With a cautious glance at the sagging roof and rotted floorboards on the front porch, he changed his opinion. Laura Bryant needed to be put into a padded cell. Anyone who would spend hard-earned cash for this place was either hiding from the law or crazy.

He heard the slamming of the back screen door and walked around the side of the house. Why did he have to be in Philadelphia last month when

Kelli's friend Laura came to visit? He should have called New Mexico and run a check on her. Union Station was his responsibility; everyone expected him to keep them safe. Now there was a psychotic living among them. He glanced down at the revolver hanging at his hip and wondered if now, after four years of being on the force, he would have to put bullets in it.

Josh rounded the back of the house and froze. Parked on the grass, close to the back door, was the dusty Jeep and horse trailer from the gas station. His gaze jerked from Logan, who was walking toward him, to the woman stepping off the back stoop. Those legs had a name, he thought, and it was Laura.

Laura's warm smile of greeting slipped as she noted the stunned expression of the police officer standing in her yard. His crystal-blue eyes sparked with recognition and astonishment. The light blue of his uniform shirt nearly matched his eyes, while his short coal-black hair looked soft and inviting. His face was tanned and classically handsome, but in a rough way. It spoke of strength and masculinity, and his sensual lower lip hinted at a more passionate side.

Her gaze drifted downward as Logan made the introductions. Broad shoulders, well-developed arms, and a chest with a silver badge pinned to it were caressed by the standard policeman's shirt. Navy pants hugged lean hips where a black leather holster held a service revolver. Colombo never looked like this!

Laura walked the few remaining steps toward him and held out her hand. "It's a pleasure to meet you, Josh. I'm sorry if Logan inconvenienced you tonight. We could manage on our own if you have some other plans." The man had to have plans, she thought. His little black book probably rivaled the phone directory.

Josh came to his senses with a thud. Her voice held a musical quality that seemed to slip down his spine and touch his soul. Her large deep-brown eyes widened as he briefly shook her outstretched hand. "The only plans I had were to help Logan help you." His questioning glance shot to the horse trailer. "I had envisioned a moving truck, though."

"I sold everything that could be easily replaced," she said. "There wasn't much left when I was done."

Josh raised an eyebrow toward Logan, who just shrugged. Wanting to put some distance between Laura and himself, Josh walked to the back of the trailer. As he lifted the bolt and opened the double doors, he heard Laura's warning shout. Two cardboard boxes tumbled out, aiming for his head. He quickly raised his arms to hold them back and grunted in pain as something bounced off his foot. He vaguely heard Logan's chuckle as he closed his eyes against the stars dancing before them.

Feeling Logan reach for one of the boxes he was still holding back, Josh hesitantly opened his eyes. Every inch of the trailer was crammed solid. Laura couldn't have fit even a toothbrush in.

"Are you all right, Josh?" she asked.

He looked down and watched as she picked up a dented toaster. "Sure, us cops are tough." He moved aside for Logan and took the remaining box down from its perch. "You just stand back and tell us what goes where, and we'll have you moved in faster that you can say Monongahela River." He saw a K on the heavy box cradled in his arm and headed for the kitchen.

Laura glanced at the retreating backs of the men and tapped her foot. An idiot could figure out which box went where, she thought. They were all marked. She clutched the toaster, walked to the Jeep, and picked up another cactus.

• • •

Josh frowned as Laura swept past him carrying a kitchen chair. He quickly realized she wasn't the type of woman who sat back and let other people do the work. She jumped right in and started grabbing boxes. The trailer was one third empty as he carefully pulled an Indian rug off two oak bureaus. He passed the rug to Logan, then removed the top drawer from the larger bureau.

He started across the yard, but his feet faltered as he looked down into the drawer. Silky undies were neatly stacked next to lacy bras. An enticing aroma of roses and sunshine rose from a decorative sachet nestled in between satiny slips. It wasn't the intimate apparel that caused him to stumble, it was what was lying on top of them. The garments cushioned a silver hand mirror, brush, and comb with turquoise stones embedded in their handles. Beside the brush was a five-by-seven silver picture frame with a photo of a young man, woman, and small child.

The woman could have been Laura, except he estimated the photo was over twenty years old. That meant the little girl in the black and white photo was Laura. She appeared to be around four. Her hair was pulled back into a ponytail, and a feathering of bangs were cut high on her small forehead. She was dressed in a flower-print dress, white anklets, and sandals. Her smile held the sweet, innocent joy only a child who was well loved and cared for could exhibit. What had happened in her young life that had changed it so drastically he wondered.

Josh climbed the stairs, heading for the bedroom Laura had indicated was hers. He knew she had grown up in foster homes, the same as Kelli, until she graduated from high school. He set the drawer down on the floor and studied the photo once more. What had happened to the smiling couple? Had they deserted Laura, or had they been taken before their time, leaving a small, frightened daughter behind?

He excused the questions as professional curiosity as he hurried past Laura in the kitchen. One fact remained in his head as he pulled another drawer out of the chest. That was one very valuable brush set for a mere newspaper reporter to own.

"Please be careful with that," Laura begged.

Logan and Josh glanced at the black steamer trunk they were pulling from the back of the Jeep. This was the first time Laura had expressed any concern over her possessions.

"What's in it?" Josh asked curiously.

A guilty flash brightened her cheeks. "Family heirlooms."

"Josh and Logan tightened their grip on the leather handles and lifted the trunk out of the Jeep. Astonishment clouded their faces as they bore its full weight. The trunk felt empty.

Laura hurried before them and held the door. After seeing them safely into the house, she rushed up the steps ahead of them. "It goes up to the third floor."

"Are you sure you want it on the third floor?" Logan asked.

She grasped her hand in front of her. "Please."

Josh noticed her discomfort and quickly reassured her. "We'll put it wherever you want it. It's your house and your—" he tested the weight of the trunk again—"heirlooms."

Laura read the unspoken question in his voice and flew up the stairs to the third floor. Quickly she opened the door to the room she had swept out earlier and stepped back. She bit her bottom lip as Josh and Logan lowered the trunk to the floor in the center of the room. "Thank you both." With a nervous gesture she ushered them from the room, then turned off the hall light and practically dragged them back down the stairs. "How about if I make something to eat and drink?"

"Something cold to drink would be great, but I'm not hungry," Logan said.

"Ditto for me," Josh said, still looking puzzled.

Laura maintained her rapid pace back to the kitchen. "It'll be ready in a jiffy."

"While you find the glasses," Logan said, following her, "I'll put the legs on the kitchen table. Josh, why don't you go set up Laura's bed for her?"

Josh glared at his friend. It would seem childish to demand to do the table, but the farther he was from Laura's bed, the better it would be for his overactive hormones. The sight of her long, tanned legs was permanently engraved in his brain. He didn't need the memory of her bed slats to drive him over the edge. He started to speak, but Logan just grinned at him and strolled into the kitchen.

Laura carried a tall glass of lemonade up to her bedroom. A muttered oath emerged from the corner of the room where Josh was battling with the oak headboard. "Need any help?"

Josh glanced up and forced a pleasant smile. The woman didn't give up, he thought. Here he was, trying to be a helping friend, while she seduced him with icy drinks and damp wisps of hair clinging to her slender neck. "Grab that end of the board and hold it still," he said.

She placed his drink on the windowsill and did as directed. The bed frame slid together without any more problems. She stepped out from between the frame as Josh carefully placed the slats across it. She helped him pick up the box spring and mattress and fit them on the framework. For the first time in five nights she'd be sleeping in her own bed. With impish delight she threw herself backward and bounced on the mattress.

Josh's determination started to crumple. His hand trembled as he raised the glass to his lips and downed all of the icy liquid.

Laura bounced once and stilled, staring at Josh's profile as he gulped the lemonade. His face held the sheen of perspiration and the beginning shadows of his beard. His head was thrown back and his eyes were closed in pleasure. She felt a faint quiver in her stomach as she realized Josh Langley was one very sexy man. He even made drinking old-fashioned lemonade seem sensual and exciting.

He lowered the empty glass and turned his head toward her.

Laura was rising from the mattress, but froze when she encountered his heated stare. Was that desire burning in his eyes? She cursed being nearsighted, and wondered if he'd consent to stay exactly like that while she rummaged through her purse for her glasses?

He frowned and pulled his gaze away from her. "Is there anything else you want done before I leave?"

So much for desire, she thought. "No, you and Logan handled everything. The rest can wait for another day. I've been up since four-thirty. All I want now is a hot shower and cool sheets."

The glass practically cracked in Josh's grip as he followed her from the room. His eyes locked on her swinging ponytail as they went back down the stairs. Logan was pushing the four wooden chairs around the table as they entered the kitchen. "Are you about ready, Logan?" he asked. "I think our hostess is dead on her feet."

"Are you going to be okay here by yourself?" Logan asked.

Laura scowled at the two men. "I've been living alone for the past ten years. Why won't I be okay in my own house?"

Josh wanted to voice his concern about the rumors of old man Peterson's ghost, but kept his mouth closed. Dark circles had formed under Laura's eyes, and her shoulders were drooping. She didn't deserve a sleepless night after the day she had put in. Besides, there weren't any such things as ghosts. "You did check the locks on both doors?" he couldn't help asking.

"Yes, sir," she snapped.

"What about the smoke detectors?" Logan asked.

"They were working fine this afternoon. So unless those little copper-top batteries aren't doing their jobs, I should survive the night."

Josh bit his cheek to prevent the chuckle from escaping. "Mrs. Billington said you're not allowed to contact her. She'll see you Sunday at the covered-dish dinner."

"Why not? What covered-dish dinner?"

"She doesn't want you to talk to her until after the scavenger hunt. That way no one can say she passed you any clues. The dinner is held in the park and it lasts all day."

"Oh. So when is the hunt?"

"It starts Friday night."

"Friday night? How are we supposed to see to find things?"

Josh glanced at Logan, then back to Laura. "Didn't anyone tell you anything about the hunt?"

"Just that you would be my partner." In a hesitant voice she added, "That is, unless you've changed your mind?"

"No, I haven't changed my mind. We're still partners." He glanced at his watch and saw it was after nine o'clock. "Okay, partner, this is how it is. The hunt lasts for thirty-six hours straight. Nonstop. I want you to lock these doors and go to bed and sleep for at least eight hours. Tomorrow night I'll stop by around six with a copy of last year's clues so you can see what we're up against."

"You mean we aren't going to be looking for leaves in the shapes of the seven wonders of the world, or a bug that has red on it?"

"Oh, Lord, an amateur! Kelli set me up with a girl scout."

Laura's temper started to rise. "I can decipher clues as well as the next guy. So, don't you worry, mister sleuth. I'll pull my weight."

Logan coughed and headed out the back door. "Good night, Laura. I'll tell Kelli you're all settled in."

Laura scowled at the swinging screen door. "Thanks, Logan." She knew he had enjoyed the exchange between herself and Josh. He deserved to choke on his laughter.

"I'm sorry, Laura," Josh said. "I didn't mean to call you an amateur. It's just that I hate to lose. What kind of an example would I set if the sheriff couldn't solve most of the clues?"

She took a deep breath and relaxed. Josh was right. It was important that he at least do well, if not win, this hunt. He was going into it handicapped by being partnered with a newcomer. "If you would bring everything you can on past hunts, I'll fix us dinner tomorrow night so we can discuss strategies."

An unexpected happiness lightened his heart. "Sounds good. I'll be here at six." He walked to the door and opened it. "Lock up and go to bed." He was outside when his voice floated back. "Can you cook?"

Laura chuckled. "You should have asked that

before you accepted," she said, then shut the solid inner door and clicked the lock.

Josh smiled into the darkness as he rounded the house. Logan, who was blocked in by the police cruiser, was leaning against his van. Josh stopped next to him and slumped against the van's rear door. "I have only one question."

Logan raised his eyebrows. "What's that?"

"What do you suppose the 'family heirloom' is?"

Both men leaned their heads back to stare up at the third floor window. Minutes went by while they considered the question, then they stiffened as a light appeared in the window.

Josh held his breath as a shadow crossed in front of the light. Two minutes later the light was extinguished, leaving only Laura's bedroom light burning. Josh dragged air into his lungs. No screams filled the night. "She must have checked on the 'heirloom.'"

"Must be valuable," Logan muttered.

"Or fragile."

"It really isn't any of our business what it is.

Josh glanced at his friend. "You're right. Families have, and are entitled to, different things they value." He pushed himself away from the van and headed for the cruiser. "See you around, Logan. Give Kelli and my goddaughter my love."

Logan opened his door and started to climb in. "Josh?"

"Yeah?"

"When you find out, tell me what the hell's in that trunk."

Two

Josh swiped at the sweat dripping into his eyes as he jogged down Main Street, glancing at the darkened shops and the occasional residence. The pale light streaming from the streetlamps shone on the clock on the steeple of the town hall. Twelve-thirty, and all was well.

At the intersection of Main and Sixth he veered right and headed up the slight incline. Sweat trickled down his back and his calves protested the grade of the hill. Now he knew why he rarely ran up Sixth Street.

After leaving Laura's earlier that night, he had headed out to Joe's Diner on the highway to grab a quick bite. He had just finished a piece of peach pie when he received word that a fight was brewing at Bronco Bill's, the local watering hole. It had been midnight before he'd returned to his apartment above his grandparents' garage. With a sigh he had thrown his keys on the counter that separated the kitchen from the living room. He'd known he was too wound up to sleep. Blaming it on the tense atmosphere at Bronco Bill's that had never developed into a physical brawl, he had headed into the bedroom to change into a pair of running shorts and a T-shirt.

Josh dragged air into his lungs as he ran, glancing from left to right. Everything looked peaceful and quiet. Houses were shrouded in darkness, with an occasional tricycle dotting the sun-baked lawns. His breathing was rapid as he wiped the dampness from his brow and stared at the house on the slight rise. Light spilling from the full moon illuminated the formidable house in which Laura slept.

Josh muttered a curse at his own foolishness as he jogged closer to the darkened house. The three massive oaks blocked most of the house from his view, but he could pick out Laura's bedroom window. Silence. The only sound he could detect was the faint barking of the Moyers' beagle over on Third Street. He silently berated his overactive imagination as he pictured Laura running out of her house straight into his arms. Dressed in a sheer negligee, her body would be trembling as she breathlessly explained how the ghost of old man Peterson had chased her around her bedroom. With the full moon, sinister house, and her flowing white attire, they could have been on the cover of one of those Gothic romances that Sanderson's Pharmacy used to stock next to the fishing magazines.

He scrutinized her house one last time, then slowly jogged past it before turning right onto Pine. It was a real shame these weren't Gothic times, he thought. In today's world women didn't need or want to be protected. They were like Laura, self-sufficient and independent. If Peterson's ghost appeared in Laura's room, Josh would bet a week's wages that she would banish the old geezer to God's acre. What would a woman like Laura Bryant need with a closet knight?

He heard a baby crying inside the Cameron

house. There was nothing unusual in that. At last count, there were seven children, but Erin and Donald could have slipped another one in there without anyone noticing. He passed their house and grinned as the kitchen light was flicked on. Someone else in town was having a difficult time sleeping.

Josh trotted onto Second Avenue, then slowed to a walk as he reached his grandparents' driveway. At the foot of the wooden stairs leading to his apartment, he stopped and dropped onto the bottom step. The humidity was high and so was the temperature. He smiled as the gentle hum of his air conditioner reached his ears. There was only one thing worse than jogging in all this heat, and that was not jogging at all. He stretched his legs out in front of him and leaned back on his elbows as his breathing slowed. He pitied the poor souls trying to sleep that night without an air conditioner or fan.

A frown drew his dark eyebrows together. Laura didn't have air conditioning, or a fan. Lord, she must be sweltering. Even without a sheet, it would be unbearable. Her nightgown would be sticking to her like a second skin, so she would probably pull it off. Damn, he thought, it was getting hotter outside. With a muttered oath Josh jumped to his feet and stormed up the stairs. Tomorrow he'd make sure Laura had a fan. It would not look good on his record if one of the town's citizens died of a heat stroke.

Laura studied her reflection in the dented toaster. Why she had bothered to put on makeup in this heat was a mystery. Her mascara was halfway off already and Josh hadn't even arrived. She grabbed a handful of tissues and wiped off the remaining makeup. Damp wisps of hair that had escaped her topknot clung to her neck and brow. She had spent the entire morning and afternoon unpacking boxes and scrubbing, and had barely had enough time to make a pot of chili for Josh's promised dinner. But the chili was bubbling on the back burner, a bowl of fresh salad was in the refrigerator, and a loaf of Italian bread was on the table. The only thing missing was Josh.

It was a quarter after six and she was ready. If Josh had shown up on time, he would have caught her dressed in a bath towel running around looking for the iron. She had unpacked every box, and still the iron was missing. It had taken her five minutes of searching through her closet to find the least wrinkled outfit. Dressed in a calf-length skirt of desert gold and brown, she blessed the latest fashion craze for the crinkled look. A sleeveless gold French knit top, sandals, and a pair of Aztec design earrings completed the outfit.

Laura pulled open the refrigerator door and plucked a juicy strawberry off the top of the dessert. Standing in front of the open door, she allowed the cold air to flow out. Her eyes closed as she bit into the succulent fruit and savored the sweet morsel.

Her gaze darted to the clock on the stove as she heard the sound of a car pulling into her driveway. He was seventeen minutes late. No one would accuse him of being overeager. She finished the berry and closed the refrigerator door.

Josh shifted the box in his arms and knocked on the back screen door. Smiling, he watched Laura walk across the kitchen toward him. She appeared to be handling the heat. In fact, she looked fresh and cool. "Sorry I'm late," he said as she opened the door.

She glanced curiously at the bulky box he was carrying. "That's okay."

"I would have been here on time, but Charlie

McPhearson dumped a truckload of hay out on the highway. It took us a while to reload it." Josh purposely left out the part about Charlie thinking he was crazy for glancing at his watch every time he threw an eighty-pound bale of hay back on the truck.

Laura noted his damp hair, clean jeans, and yellow pullover. He must have showered and changed before coming. That was a good sign. "It was awfully nice of you to help."

"All part of the job." Josh glanced around the kitchen and noticed the improvement. It looked like Laura was settled in her new home. The tantalizing smell coming from the stove reminded him that he had skipped lunch in order to pick up a fan for her. He placed the box on the counter. "I believe it's proper for a guest to bring his hostess a token of appreciation. I thought about a bottle of wine, but I wasn't sure what we would be having."

"Chili."

"Hot and spicy?"

Laura picked up on his hopeful tone and smiled. "I wasn't sure if you would like it hot, so I tried to calm it down. I'm not sure if I succeeded."

A spark gleamed in his blue eyes as he leaned against the counter. "I love it hot."

Laura's heart rate quickened at the roughness in his voice. Were they still talking about chili? Of course he was still talking about chili, she told herself. What else could he possibly be referring to? She pulled her gaze from his and studied the box on the counter. "A fan?"

Josh saw the confusion that clouded her eyes and grimaced. What in the hell was he doing? This was Laura, Kelli's friend, he was talking to. She was a lady and deserved to be treated as such. "With all the unpacking we did last night, I didn't remember seeing a fan."

"You didn't have to go out and buy one for me. I

had it on my shopping list right under shower-curtain rings and window shades."

Josh watched in amusement as she gleefully ripped into the box and pulled out the twelve-inch oscillating silver beauty. The expression of anticipation on her face reminded him of an eager child on Christmas morning. He should have wrapped it, he thought.

With careful fingers Laura unhooked the manufacturer's tag and plugged in the fan. A touch of a button and a gentle breeze stirred to life. She closed her eyes, arched her neck and allowed the cool air to caress her moist skin. A soft sigh escaped her. "Heaven."

Josh froze as heat pounded through his veins. He couldn't take his eyes off her. Tendrils of hair that had escaped her topknot were dancing in the breeze. Her face was a mask of pure sensual pleasure. With her head thrown back and her lips parted, she looked as if she were waiting for a lover's kiss.

He was in trouble. Big trouble. Trouble with a capital T. This wasn't what was supposed to happen. He had bought the fan so *he* could sleep better knowing she was somewhat cool. The previous night he had tossed and turned in his solitary bed, haunted by visions of Laura trying to sleep without so much as a puff of cool air. He had tinted the cool air bluer with his curses, till the pale light of dawn crept into his room. Untangling himself from his jumbled sheets, he'd clicked off his air conditioner and opened the windows. Guilt made a lousy bed partner. He'd finally drifted off to sleep, wondering if he was feeling guilty about being cool or about having a few fantasies about his partner for the scavenger hunt.

He came back to the present as a puzzled Laura repeated herself. "Thank you again, Josh." What in the world was he thinking to cause his eyes to glaze over like that? she wondered. She reached into a cabinet and pulled down two mismatched bowls. "Did you bring any of last year's clues with you?"

He held the bowls as she filled them with thick, bubbling chili. "I have the past two years' lists. I'll let you read them after dinner only if this chili tastes as great as it looks.

Laura set the salad and two bottles of dressing on the table. "And if it doesn't?"

He focused on the gentle sway of her hips as she walked back to the refrigerator. "I don't think I'll be disappointed."

She returned to the table with two cans of cold beer and two tall glasses. One glass boasted the image of the Lone Ranger, the other Tonto. "Is beer okay or are you on duty?"

Amused, he asked, "Entertain cops a lot?"

"You're the first." She flashed him a brilliant smile. "I'm addicted to Ed McBain's 87th Precinct novels, and the cops in them don't drink while on duty." After a moment's pause, she added, "At least they aren't supposed to."

"I've read those novels too." Okay, he thought. So they had something else in common besides hot chili and cold beer. "Beer is fine. I'm not on duty. My deputy, Cal, is handling anything that comes in tonight." He accepted the frosty can and helped himself to the salad.

"Will Cal be on duty the entire weekend?" she asked.

"Yep. I'll have to keep a radio with me, though. The whole town goes crazy during the hunt, and occasionally we have to step in to help resolve a dispute."

"You mean a fight?"

"The last actual fistfight we had was three years ago."

"What happened?" she asked, fascinated.

Josh debated changing the subject but decided against it. Even if the incident still made him uncomfortable with memories of his own past, to Laura it would just be an example of life in Union Station. "Christina Burke's older brother, Geoffrey," he began, "found out she had entered the hunt with Dave Parker. The Burkes are the oldest and wealthiest family around these parts. Dave works as a truck driver for the local feed mill."

Laura poured Italian dressing over her salad and raised an eyebrow when Josh didn't continue. "So?"

Josh sighed. He had hoped that explanation would satisfy her. "Union Station doesn't actually have train tracks, but if it did, you could say Dave came from the wrong side.

She thoughtfully chewed a tomato slice. "Rich girl, poor boy?"

"That's putting it mildly." It was more than just money. It was a complete separation of the classes. Upper and rock-bottom.

Laura caught the edge in Josh's voice. "I hope this Christina set her brother straight."

"Oh, sure. By the next week Daddy had bought her a sports car and packed her off to Philadelphia to live with her aunt and a 'better class' of people."

"You're joking!"

"Nope. Last I heard she was married to some hotshot banker."

Laura shivered at the emotion that vibrated in Josh's voice. He was disturbed by something more than an ill-fated partnership for a scavenger hunt. She had met and disliked girls like Christina in school, and she personally thought Dave was better off without her. So what was Josh's problem?

Josh shook off the old feeling of insecurity and grinned as he scooped up his first spoonful of chili. "You said you calmed this down from your usual."

"I think so." She held her breath as he tasted the chili. Her teeth sank into her lower lip as he swallowed and quickly grabbed his glass of beer and downed half of it.

Gasping for breath, he smiled ridiculously. In a choked voice suitable for a fire-breathing dragon, he said, "I think I'm in love."

Laura pushed the glasses up her nose and studied the list in front of her. Some of the clues were easy, like "equipment for a solar dryer." She had guessed clothespin before seeing the answer. Josh had written in as many answers as he could remember, which was quite a few. Laura kept her head down and glanced over the rim of her glasses at him as he busily washed her dishes.

She still couldn't believe he had eaten three helpings of her chili. Where did he put it? His shoulders were broad and his chest and arms bulged in all the right places. Soft worn denim hugged his narrow waist and lean hips. There was not one ounce of excess fat anywhere on his gorgeous body.

Her gaze shifted back to the list of last year's clues, and she silently sighed. With his light-blue eyes and his having lived his entire thirty years in Pennsylvania, chances were Josh didn't have one drop of Navaho blood running through his veins. In the past ten years she had learned to be very selective about friends she brought home.

When she had conjured up a guardian spirit ten years before on top of a lonely mesa, she'd been thrilled and excited. She had climbed that mesa the week after graduating from high school, unsure of which direction her life should go. Within a blinding flash of light her guardian spirit had come to her, along with the decision to attend college and major in writing. Her one hazy glimpse of him had revealed the hulking figure of an Indian chief dressed in full warrior gear. For the first six months she had walked around with a silly smile plastered on her face. She had her very own guardian spirit to guide her through life. What could go wrong?"

Trouble started the night she invited Patrick O'Toole into her apartment after a casual date to the movies. When Patrick took her in his arms, she went willingly. As his mouth claimed hers, though, the walls started to vibrate. By the time the sofa had jerked a few inches away from the wall, Patrick had run from the apartment as if the hounds of hell were after him. In the months that followed, Laura brought home assorted dates to the same disastrous results, although her guardian spirit was slightly more lenient with a male who had Navaho blood.

One year after acquiring her Indian chief, Laura found herself on top of the same mesa trying desperately to send him back. He wouldn't go. She spent the next five years researching ancient Navaho ceremonies. She found plenty of references to summoning a guardian spirit, but not one word on how to get rid of one. Laura Ann Bryant was stuck with a crazy Indian chief who had morals. She was twenty-eight and destined to die a virgin.

Last year she had given up dating altogether. Every time she began to like an interesting male and the physical side of the relationship started to develop, the walls would shake. Thunder and lightning appeared out of nowhere, or some other strange occurrence broke the mood. She had hoped the move across the country would discourage Chief Snuggle Bear from coming, but he'd been with her every mile and was now comfortably settled in a room on the third floor.

With a last lingering glance at Josh's swaying rear as he wiped down the counter, she bit back a groan and returned to the list. "Most of it seems simple enough."

Josh turned around and smiled at the picture she made. She looked like a prim and proper schoolmarm with her hair piled up on top of her head and a pair of glasses perched on the end of her nose. "About three fourths of the clues are everyday items that could be found anywhere," he said. "It's the other fourth we have to worry about. Some of those are single items, in which case there's only one of them and there is a total of thirty-seven teams going after them this year." He hung the dishcloth over the faucet and sat back down across from her.

"Are teams allowed to split up?"

"No. Starting tomorrow night at six, when we pick up the list of clues at the park, we have to stay together for thirty-six hours. The hunt officially ends at six o'clock Sunday morning."

Laura glanced at the list of seventy-five clues in her hand. Roughly twenty items were one-of-a-kind or pertained only to the town of Union Station. That left about fifty-five ordinary items, if she could decipher the clues. "How would anyone know if we split up?"

"There's a citizens patrol whose job is to make sure we don't. Take my word for it, they're worse than the actual hunters."

"How?" she asked, intrigued.

"As hunters we drive around in clear view, collecting as many items as we can. The patrol splits up, hides, and waits for some hunter to break the rules."

"So not only are we the hunters, we're also the hunted?"

"Got it in one. The patrol can't touch us as long as we obey the rules." Josh held up his hand and started to tick off the rules on his fingers. "Under no circumstances are we allowed to split up. Under no circumstances are we allowed to purchase any item on the list. All items must be *found*, not *bought.* Only under a medical emergency are we allowed to converse with a member of the citizens patrol, or another hunter. Under no circumstances are we allowed to beg, borrow, or steal another hunter's items. After you have an item in your possession, it's yours until the judging. After which time, we must return all items to their original state." He held up his thumb and said the last rule. "Precisely at six o'clock Sunday morning we must be indoors. This is our designated rest period before the judging begins as noon at the park. If a hunter wishes to go to church, he is to be escorted by a member of the citizens patrol. All entries must be at the park at precisely twelve or be disqualified."

Laura's mouth fell open in total amazement. "Did you memorize all that?"

"After overseeing the hunt for the past four years, the rules have been drummed into my head. I've broken up my share of arguments between desperate hunters and overzealous citizens.

A feeling of dread swept through Laura. When the scavenger hunt was first brought up, she'd thought it would be fun and exciting. But seeing the sober look on Josh's face, she realized that this was a serious contest. "This may sound naive, but what do the winners win?"

"The winning team receives a free dinner at Emma's Place, a one-year free subscription to *The Union Station Review*, and one free oil change and lube at Harley's gas station."

Laura blinked. That was it? The way Josh was sprouting rules and regulations, she'd figured on a thousand-dollar savings bond at least. Maybe a new Chevy pickup truck or a guest spot on Johnny Carson. Last month when she'd visited Kelli, they had eaten at Emma's Place. It had been a Wednesday night and the only entree on the blackboard was meat loaf, but they did have a choice between apple pie or walnut cake for dessert.

Josh sat mesmerized as Laura tilted her head back and laughed. His hand tightened around his glass as the sound of her mirth touched someplace deep in his soul. How could her laugh be both seductive and innocent? He shifted uncomfortably in his chair and decided the more distance he put between himself and Laura, the better off he'd be. Otherwise, he might do something incredibly stupid, like kiss her. Glowering at her, he snapped, "I know it's not a whole hell of a lot to win, but it's the prestige of winning that counts."

Laura abruptly stopped laughing. Oh-oh, she thought. Now she'd done it. She'd just offended the entire town, and the sheriff looked mad enough to run her out of it on a rail. "I'm not laughing at the prizes," she said gently.

"You're not?"

"No. I was laughing for the sheer fun of it, just like the scavenger hunt. The whole town goes crazy for one weekend a year, just for the fun of it." She noticed he didn't look too convinced with her explanation. "It's a wonderful idea. When you started to list all the rules, it seemed to take the fun out of it."

"And you would rather do it for the fun of it than for the prizes?"

"If Mrs. Billington didn't assign covering the scavenger hunt as a participant, I probably would have entered it *just for the fun of it.*"

"Are you out to win or to have a good time?" he asked curiously.

She lifted her chin, and her nose wrinkled as she stared down it. "I plan on having a wonderful time *winning* the hunt."

Josh finished his beer and stood. "Then it's a good thing we're on the same team, because I plan on winning too." He pushed in his chair and asked, "Do you have any other questions before I leave?"

Laura took off her glasses and stood also. She wanted to ask him to stay longer, but obviously he was in a hurry to go. "Should I meet you in the park tomorrow night?"

"No, I'll pick you up about five-thirty." He started toward the door, then stopped and turned around. "Thanks for dinner. It was nice to eat with someone who appreciates the finer things in life."

Following him to the door, she smiled. He considered hot chili and cold beer a delicacy. She halted a foot away from him and gazed up. "Thank you for the fan, Josh. It was really sweet of you."

Josh stared down at her beautiful, innocent face and felt a burning desire clear down to his toes. His heart pounded and he started to reach for her before he became aware of his own intent. *He was going to kiss her!* With a sudden jerk he backed into the screen door. What in the hell had come over him? He didn't go around kissing the fair citizens of Union Station. He was there to serve and protect, not harass and molest.

Laura watched bewildered as Josh backed away. She had been close enough to read the expression on his face. He had been ready to kiss her. "Josh?"

"I've got to run. Make sure you lock up tight. They're predicting thundershowers later tonight." He opened the door and stepped outside. Clouds were already rolling in and a slight breeze stirred the air. "I'll see you tomorrow night."

He had taken a few hurried strides toward his car when she called out, "Josh?"

He paused and looked over his shoulder at her standing alone and bewildered on her back stoop.

"You won't regret having me for a partner," she said. "We'll win the hunt."

He flashed her a boyish grin as he climbed into a gleaming white Corvette. "I hope so, because I've already made an appointment for my oil change and lube at Harley's." Silently, though, he did regret having her for a partner. How was he going to stay in her company for thirty-six hours straight without kissing her? With a wave of his hand he slowly backed down her driveway and into the gathering dusk.

Laura returned his wave and watched until the low-slung white car was out of sight. Then she stopped grinding her back teeth and stormed into the kitchen. The slamming of the screen door vibrated through the house as she planted her feet at the bottom of the stairs. "Chief Snuggle Bear, I want your butt down here this instant!" She counted to five, then continued to lecture the empty stairwell. "What did you do to Josh? I couldn't see anything, but I know you had to do something. He was about to kiss me."

She clenched her fist in frustration and pounded the faded flower wallpaper on the hall wall. "Dammit, Chief, I wanted that kiss." Tears filled her eyes as she stared up at the hanging light in the hall, which blinked on and off with each thump of her fist. Great, the wiring in the house had probably been installed by Edison.

Her shoulders slumped as she turned away and headed for the den. "Fine, have it your way. I'll die a lonely old spinster. But I'll tell you one thing, you feather-sprouting creature, you better take care of this house." She turned around and shook a finger at the empty living room. "I purposely bought this place for you. Not too many guardian spirits could claim they have a room of their own, let alone an entire third floor. So you'd better make sure that it doesn't burn down, leak, or become infested with termites."

At the double glass doors leading to the study she stopped, straightened her shoulders, and glared. "And if by some chance you do see old man Peterson's ghost walking these halls, you'd better send him packing. It's bad enough to share the house with you, but I draw the line at ghosts." With a violent twist of the crystal doorknob she flung open the door, stepped through, and slammed it shut. Turning her back on whatever was on the other side of those glass doors, she headed for the piles of books scattered around the floor and the empty bookshelves lining one entire wall.

Josh pulled his car over to the curb and turned off the headlights. With a weary sigh he glanced at the clock in the dash. Midnight. He turned the windshield wipers down to low and studied the house on the hill. Everything looked fine. So why had he dashed out in the middle of a thunderstorm to check on Laura?

The rain had slowed from a torrent to a steady downpour, but the lightning and thunder were at their peak. He reached up and swiped at the drops of water running off his hair. This was ridiculous. He should be home in bed trying to catch a good night's sleep before the scavenger hunt.

He took one last look at the house and froze. Lightning lit up the sky, and silhouetted on Laura's roof was an Indian. At least in that split second it looked like an Indian, with his arms stretched toward the heavens. In a blink of an eye he was gone. Josh frantically wiped at the fog forming on his windshield and stared at the roof.

Another bolt of lightning illuminated the night. Nothing. Josh's curses filled the car, along with the crack of thunder. Now he was imagining things. What in the hell was happening to him? This was all Laura's fault. Her and her sweet innocence and tempting lips.

Twenty minutes later Josh turned the headlights back on and headed home. He needed a vacation. A shudder slid down his back at the thought of a town council hearing on whether or not the sheriff was imagining Indians. It must have been a tree branch or a stray rain cloud passing in front of the moon. Laura's roof was three stories high, the wind was gusting at forty miles per hour, and lightning bolts were striking everywhere. No person in his right mind would climb up on Laura's roof, be it doctor, lawyer, or Indian chief.

Three

"Hurry up, Laura, move it."

Laura jumped out of the pickup truck and hurried after Josh. "Where's the fire?" she muttered, glaring at his back.

Josh impatiently tapped his sneaker-clad foot and waited for her to catch up. "We're behind schedule."

"How could a scavenger hunt have a schedule?"

A quick glance at his watch had him racing around the side of a charming yellow Victorian house. "I worked out a timetable. Out of the thirty-six hours, I allowed us seven hours for sleep. That means we must find three and a half items per hour to obtain everything on the list."

Laura gazed around the carefully manicured backyard. "How do we find half an item?"

Josh scowled over his shoulder at her and mumbled something she couldn't hear.

"Well, you don't have to get snippy. I'm not the one who threw us off schedule by driving into those hedges."

He planted his hands on his hips and faced her. "I ran into those hedges because you broke my concentration by screaming like a banshee."

"Of course I screamed. I had just seen a bush sprout legs and walk down the street."

"That was only Sylas."

"You knew that bush?"

"No, I know the man. He's the head of the citizens patrol."

"Did you hit your head when we flattened that hedge? That man was wearing full camouflage gear. He even had his face painted green and black." Laura's eyes widened and her voice rose in wonder. "He had more tree branches attached to his body than Sherwood Forest."

Josh suppressed the laugh threatening to erupt. She was cute when riled. He knew it wasn't all her fault they had been engaged in the hunt for two hours and had only one item to show for it. If he hadn't been thinking of how cute she looked in jeans, he might not have jerked the wheel and plowed down ten feet of the Wilsons' hedges when she screamed. "Sylas is totally harmless," he said. "He was dressed like that to spy on us."

"Oh." When Josh had told her that some of the patrol hid to spy on them, she'd envisioned them in darkened doorways or peering out of suspiciously parked cars. Not dressed like shrubbery. Lord, she hoped there weren't any stray dogs around. "Are there any other bushes I should know about?"

Josh grabbed her hand and pulled her into the middle of the lawn. "No, Sylas is the only bush. But keep your eyes open for Harley. He's partial to hiding in garbage cans. The ones I'm not sure about are Sylas's twin sons. They just turned eighteen and are eligible to become members of the patrol, but no one knows what they'll be wearing."

Laura was mulling over that piece of information when Josh tilted the top of a birdbath and dumped the water out. "What are you doing?"

"Getting the next item. What does it look like I'm doing?"

She glanced around uneasily. "Whose house is this?"

"My grandparents'." He picked up the empty concrete bowl and grunted. "Laura, pick up the base and let's go."

"You just can't take your grandparents' bird-bath."

"Laura, please," he implored.

"Yoo-hoo, Josh!"

Laura and Josh turned and watched an elderly woman hurry across the yard toward them. "Hello, Grams," Josh called. "We're taking your birdbath, this is Laura, and we have to go."

Laura gasped at his rudeness, but Josh's grandmother chuckled. "It's a pleasure meeting you, Laura," she said. "Stop back when you have a chance to stay." She held out a brown paper bag. "I packed you some cookies. They're your favorite, Josh, peanut butter. Do you like peanut butter cookies, Laura?"

Josh groaned, struggling with the heavy birdbath, and clamped his teeth down on the brown bag. He motioned Laura to follow and headed back toward the truck.

Laura hoisted the base and smiled. "Thank you, and I love peanut butter cookies."

She was halfway across the yard when Josh's grandmother yelled, "I hope you and Josh win. I have a tenspot riding on you."

Laura bit her lip to stop the laughter. Josh's sweet elderly grandmother had bet ten dollars on them. She wondered if Uncle Sam knew how she was spending her social security check. "I'm sure we will," she called back, then mischievously added, "that is, if Josh stops running into hedges."

"Is that why there are branches sticking out of

the bumper of the truck? I feared he might have run poor Sylas down."

"No, Sylas is fine. I've got to go, it's been nice meeting you."

Ida Langley chuckled as Laura disappeared around the side of the house. Josh had finally brought a girl home. Granted, it was only for a moment, and it was only to borrow her birdbath, but beggars couldn't be choosers. She'd be celebrating her eighty-third birthday next month, and the way Josh was moving, she'd be pushing up daisies before she'd be bouncing a great-grandchild on her knee.

She pulled a lace hanky from the bosom of her dress and dabbed at the moisture gathering in her eyes. Her steps were slow and measured as she crossed the yard and entered the house. She smiled fondly at her husband sleeping in his favorite chair with the newspaper in his lap. With fingers that shook from age, she dug through her knitting basket. Somewhere in there was the cutest pattern for a baby sweater.

Laura glanced up from the plastic-covered menu she was reading and said, "I still think you were rude to your grandmother."

"My grandmother understands about the scavenger hunt. She didn't expect us to stay for a cup of tea." Josh replaced his menu in the metal stand between the salt and pepper shakers. "If I promise to apologize to her the minute the hunt is over, will you stop glaring at me?"

Laura's menu joined his in the holder. "I haven't been glaring." A friendly smile tilted up the corners of her mouth as a waitress stopped at their table.

The waitress raised a finely arched eyebrow in Laura's direction, then turned her back and smiled seductively at Josh. "'Evening, Josh. Are you ready to order?"

Josh shifted uncomfortably at the waitress's obvious interest. He rarely stopped at the diner when Beth was working. It was too difficult to swallow food when the woman kept drooling over him, as if he were dessert. He had hoped having Laura along would discourage Beth. "Laura, did you decide yet?"

Laura read the silent plea in Josh's gaze. She reached across the table and covered one of his hands with hers. Her voice purred as she whispered loud enough for the hovering waitress to hear, "I decided a long time ago what I wanted."

He grinned at the twinkle in her eye and clasped her small hand. "Later, darling. Right now we have company."

Her eyebrows rose in question as to what they'd be doing *later*. His grip tightened as she tried to pull her hand away. She turned her head, encountered the hostile glare of the waitress, and gave her her order.

Josh gave his own order, then watched as Beth stomped off to another table. He squeezed Laura's hand. "Promise not to hit me and I'll give this back to you."

"Old girlfriend?" she asked, amused.

"Lord, no." At Laura's questioning glance, he shrugged. "She's very persistent."

Laura studied his stony expression and could have sworn a tinge of red had swept up his cheeks. Then again, it could be the lighting in the diner. Mr. Protector of the Law had an admirer. Who in the hell was she kidding? she asked herself. With Josh's looks, he had to have a complete cheering section. So why was he acting embarrassed by the fact?

Recalling that he still held her hand—and that

her fingers seemed to be melting from the heat radiating from him—she tugged gently against his grasp. "You can let go of me now. She's out of sight."

Josh released her and mumbled, "Thanks." Turning around, he studied the other customers in the diner. He recognized a couple of the patrons and a few truckers. The rest looked to be just passing through. At twelve-thirty in the morning the diner was one third full. Josh had purposely chosen the farthest booth from anyone. "Let's see the list again."

Laura pulled the folded pages from her over-stuffed tote bag and handed it to Josh. While he was scanning the list, she placed a thesaurus and a dictionary on the table. Digging deeper into the bag, she located her glasses and slipped them on.

Josh scowled at the list. "We've got only eight items so far."

"Yes, but we've identified another five that I have at home. That makes thirteen."

He smiled as pencils and pads of paper joined her growing pile. She was efficient and had come prepared. "Let's go over these one by one and see what we can come up with."

"'Tool used to get cows out of the corn.'" Laura sighed and stared out the window at the pickup truck Josh had borrowed from his father for the hunt. A heavy canvas tarp was strapped across the bed of the truck, covering the items they had found so far. Josh had explained that if you saw what the other hunters had found, you could figure out more clues. "I don't know, Josh. The only thing I can think of is a scarecrow, but isn't that to keep the crows out of the corn?"

"Yeah, and I've never heard of a scare*cow*. Maybe it's a misprint?"

"Mrs. Billington doesn't strike me as the kind not

to proofread, especially on something this important." Laura grabbed the thesaurus and looked up
'tool.' She scanned the list of words, then looked up
'cow' and 'corn.'

Josh thanked Beth as she placed a cup of coffee
and a glass of iced tea on the table. He stirred
sugar into his coffee and studied Laura. She was
bound and determined to prove to him the books
weren't a waste of time, after he had laughed at her
for bringing them along. Whoever heard of winning a scavenger hunt with books? It took common sense, hard work, and a keen analytical
mind. Damn, but didn't she look cute with her
glasses sliding down her nose, which she'd planted
in the book? A person could see the gears of her
mind turning as she worried her lower lip with
perfectly white teeth. With effort, he wrenched his
gaze from that gorgeous lip. "Did you find anything?"

"Did you ever hear of a person getting milk in
their bunion?"

Amazed, he asked, "Is that what the book told
you?"

"The books don't tell me anything. They suggest."

"May I *suggest* that you put the books away and
concentrate on the list of clues? We still have
eighty-seven to figure out."

Laura pushed her glasses back up her nose and
reached for the second sheet of clues. "I wouldn't
have figured you for one of those Neanderthals
whose total reading experience consisted of the
letters to the editor of *Playboy*."

"I'm not." A mischievous smile flashed across
Josh's face. "I look at the pictures too."

She tried to stop her laughter, but couldn't.
She'd walked right into that one.

Josh felt his body tighten with desire as her

laughter washed over him. Why this woman? he wondered. She was pretty in a healthy sort of way, but he'd known prettier. Her eyes were large and so dark, it was hard to tell where the irises started. Wavy shoulder-length brown hair boasted golden highlights from hours out in the sun. Her skin was soft, tanned, and flawless, but her most compelling feature was her mouth. The upper lip was curved and gave the appearance of sweetness. Her lower lip was full, rich, and lush. Since she had the fascinating habit of sinking her teeth into it, it was usually moist and had the look of just being kissed. It was that lower lip that was driving him out of his mind.

Laura's laughter trailed off when she encountered the heat of Josh's stare. With her glasses perched on her nose, she had no chance of misreading his desire. He wasn't thinking of clues, books, or even cows in the corn. A warm tingling sensation settled in the bottom of her stomach and her lips softly parted. Lord, if she felt like this just from a look, what would happen if he actually kissed her? *Nuclear meltdown!*

Josh and Laura jerked back in their seats and swung their flushed faces toward the waitress as she loudly thumped their plates down on the table, breaking the spell. Josh cleared his throat. "Thanks, Beth."

With fingers that trembled, Laura grabbed a napkin and busied herself adjusting it on her lap. Her mumbled "thanks" was lost on the annoyed waitress stomping away.

Josh studied Laura's bent head and sighed. The feelings he was experiencing toward her were mutual. Now what was he supposed to do? He could barely fight his own urge to kiss her senseless, but when her eyes had turned dreamy and soft, he'd nearly dragged her over the table and into his arms. Great! he thought derisively. Wouldn't that impress the town council? He could see the headlines now—*sheriff loses battle with hormones and attacks innocent citizen in diner.* He quelled another sigh and said, "Would you please pass the ketchup?"

Laura handed him the bottle and wondered if she was imagining the tension hovering over the table. How could he eat his dinner as if nothing were wrong when she would have choked on her first French fry? She wanted the kiss that he had promised with his eyes.

She picked up the list of clues and studied them, but her mind remained fixed on Josh. He was ruggedly handsome, with his coal-black hair cut conservatively short because of his job. His square jaw was covered with a slight shadow. Since he'd been clean-shaven when he picked her up seven hours earlier, he must be one of those men who had to shave twice a day. He oozed authority, even without the badge. His light-blue eyes held both humor and intelligence, and his mouth was strong with a sensual lower lip. Put it all together and he could have set Hollywood on its ear. Women probably flocked around him constantly, so why did he seem embarrassed by Beth's obvious interest?

"Your hamburger is getting cold."

She glanced up into his concerned eyes. "Thanks, I was concentrating." It wasn't a lie. She *was* concentrating, just not on the clues.

"Come up with anything?" he asked.

"I think so." She quickly bit into her hamburger and studied the list. Come on, she thought. There had to be an easy one here somewhere. Her prayer was answered as she read the thirty-fourth clue. "Do you know where we could find a rabbit's foot?"

"Not really. What's the clue?"

"'Luck comes your way but it's a rabbit's gloomy day.'"

"Good job. Only eighty-six more to go."

Laura grinned as she wrote "rabbit's foot" in the margin next to the clue. "Don't count your chickens, we have to find a rabbit's foot yet."

"Don't you worry, I'll find a rabbit's foot." Not to be outdone by a newspaper reporter, Josh picked up the first page and began reading.

By the time they had finished dessert almost an hour had passed and they had deciphered another twelve clues. Now all they had to do was figure out the other seventy-four.

Laura lightly tapped the lid of a garbage can and whispered, "Hello, Harley."

"Shhhhh!" Josh hissed. "Laura, what are you doing?"

"Saying hello to Harley."

Josh glanced at the dented and rusted trash can. "Is Harley really in there?"

"How should I know? I've never met him."

"Laura, is there a man in that garbage can?"

"I don't know. You told me to be quiet and not to make a sound. Banging garbage-can lids around could raise quite a ruckus."

"If you don't know if anyone is in there, why are you talking to it?"

"Because you told me Harley hangs out in garbage cans and I didn't want to appear stuck-up and not at least say hello to him."

Josh shifted his toolbox to his left hand and grabbed Laura's hand with his right. "Let's go before someone sees us and figures out what we're going for. You don't have to talk to every garbage can we run across. Harley would understand."

Laura had to take two steps for every one of his as they hurried between a group of houses. She bumped into him as he stopped suddenly in front of a white picket gate.

"Here it is." He opened up his toolbox and handed her a flashlight. "You hold the light while I work on the hinges."

She pointed the light on the top of the gate and watched as Josh unscrewed the first hinge from the post. "Can I at least ask whose gate this is?"

"Sure, it's Reverend Pauly's." The beam of light bounced across the yard toward the house. At the sudden darkness, Josh's screwdriver slipped out of the screw and nicked his hand. "Ouch! Laura, what are you doing?"

"You mean to tell me we're stealing a minister's gate?"

Josh grabbed the flashlight and shone it on the back of his hand. No blood. "We're not stealing anything, Laura. The rules clearly state that after the judging we must put this gate back *exactly* as it was."

She took the light back and shone it on the partially unscrewed hinge. "If my soul rots in purgatory, it's all your fault."

He chuckled softly as he unscrewed the bottom hinge and picked up the gate. "Grab the toolbox and follow me back to the truck." He took two steps, then stopped and turned around. "And for Pete's sake, don't talk to any more garbage cans."

Laura made a face at his back. Halfway to the truck she stopped and wished a pleasant evening to a flowering rosebush, just in case Sylas had a complete wardrobe of shrubbery.

Josh held back his smile as he slid the gate under the tarp and Laura climbed into the cab of the truck. He had just gotten behind the wheel when she sucked in a sharp breath. "Look, Josh!"

He swung his head around and watched as two people crossed the dimly lit street, struggling with a bathtub. "That's Frank and Mary. A bathtub must be one of the items we haven't deciphered yet."

Laura mentally ran through the unsolved clues. "I don't think so. I would have to check the list again, but the closest thing to a bathtub that we've come up with is a birdbath."

He watched as the couple disappeared between two houses. Where did they get the tub? Frank and Mary were a middle-aged couple whose children were all grown, married, and having babies of their own. Ever since their youngest had left the nest, they had been acting like newlyweds and creating quite a stir on their bowling team. Josh secretly thought it was cute, and had even turned his back the time he'd caught them parking at the local lovers' lane.

"We'll check the list out later," he said, "but we have one more stop before we can catch a few hours sleep."

"I don't know, Josh. It sounds too dangerous."

"Nonsense, it will be a piece of cake."

Josh held his breath and gripped the facade of the steeple tighter. He was crazy, no doubt about it. Why did he have to play Mister Macho Man in front of Laura? It really was going to be something when he splattered his macho brains all over the sidewalk four floors below. He glanced over his shoulder at a white-faced Laura standing on the roof of town hall, and sent her a reassuring smile. So who was going to reassure him? Maybe he should have gotten the hour hand off the town clock before he heisted the minister's gate.

With a silent prayer Josh maneuvered his toes along the three-inch-wide ledge. He felt the rope Laura had insisted he tie around his waist snag on the fancy woodwork as he turned the corner. Muttering a curse, he released his hold on the woodwork with one hand and gently shook the rope.

Laura breathed a sigh of relief as the rope unhooked. She wished she could see how he was doing, but she would have to go down to the street and look up. For the fifth time she berated herself for deciphering the sixteenth clue, "Mickey's little one for all the cosmos to view." It could only be the hour hand from the clock on top of the town hall. The only problem was, it was four floors up and on a steeple. "Josh?"

His muffled "yeah" came from the front of the steeple.

"I vote we forget this one."

Josh's hand slipped on the wrench he was using to loosen the end cap on the clock. "Why?"

Laura tightened her hold on the rope connected to a vent pipe and his waist. "It's too dangerous, you're tired, and you might slip."

Was that concern in her voice? he wondered. "I already have the cap off."

"We can come back after you're rested and bring a ladder."

"Too late. Frank and Mary are standing in the street watching me. We have to get it now or lose it." Josh slipped the end cap into his jeans pocket and reached for the minute hand. Sweat broke out across his brow as he maneuvered thirty pounds of wrought iron off its gear. His calves were cramping from standing on his toes, and there was nowhere to lay the four-foot-long piece of metal. "Laura, I have to pass the minute hand to you. Do you think you could manage about thirty pounds?"

Laura walked close to the steeple and the edge of the building. "Of course I can handle it." She glanced down and noticed that a small crowd was gathering in front of the town hall. It was four o'clock in the morning. Didn't anyone sleep in this town? "Please be careful, Josh."

He grabbed the ornamental side molding with one hand, the minute hand with the other, and slowly shuffled back toward Laura. With extreme care he maneuvered the iron hand until she could reach it. "Careful, it's heavy."

Laura grabbed the thing with both hands and slowly lowered it to the roof. Dismayed, she watched as Josh eased back around the corner, out of sight again. She had noticed the moisture clinging to his forehead, the trembling of his legs, and the white-knuckled grip he had on the molding. Why should he be the one to put himself in danger? she asked herself. They were partners. They were supposed to share either the victory or the defeat. That meant they should share the danger and the fun.

She took a deep breath, wiped her moist hands on the seat of her jeans, and climbed up two feet to stand on the ledge. Her hands went wild until they connected with the molding. Sucking in a deep breath, she flattened herself against the steeple.

"Laura?"

Over the pounding of her heart she said, "I'm on the ledge with you."

"Get down!"

"I'll be more than glad to get down just as soon as you pass me the hour hand." She shuffled over and glanced around the corner. The color left her face as she spotted Josh balanced on his toes, removing the hour hand. The only thing he had to hold on to was the metal shaft with its gears.

Josh's own face paled when he saw Laura. If she lost her balance and fell backwards, she'd land on the roof just two feet below. But if she fell forward, she'd go right over the side of the building. "Please, Laura, get down."

"Pass me the hand."

"It will be too heavy for you to handle while you are balancing on the ledge."

Her voice lost its musical quality. "Are you saying I can't pull my own weight in this partnership?"

"Dammit, Laura. This is not the time to discuss our partnership. Just get back on the roof and take the hour hand when I pass it to you."

"No. Pass it to me now and I'll get down."

Josh studied her face in the pale glow cast by two spotlights pointing at the clock. It looked ghostly white, but serious. He muttered something about women's lib and slid the three-foot iron hand along the edge.

Watching, Laura bit her lip and wondered how she was going to hang on and pick up the heavy hand. Josh shuffled to the corner where she waited, glared at her, grabbed hold of the molding, and started to pick up the hour hand. He froze at the sound of a loud *CRACK!*

His eyes widened as he stared at the piece of molding that had broken away from the steeple, still clutched in his hand. He was tilting backward into space when Laura made a desperate grab for his outstretched hand.

Her weight had been distributed to take the load of the iron hand, not Josh's body in motion. She felt her sneakers slide as she tightened her grip on the woodwork and Josh's wrist.

Instinct told Josh to grasp Laura's hand. Fear told him that he was attached to a rope that would break his fall before he hit the ground. Laura wasn't. He felt her grip tighten as screams from below reached his ears.

Laura's arm felt as if it were being pulled out of the socket as she screamed one word in desperation. "Chief!" With the strength of ten women she slowly hauled Josh up until he regained his balance.

Josh threw the hour hand on the roof and grabbed a solid piece of molding. Balanced again, he took a deep breath and jumped the three feet to the roof. Without saying a word he walked over to where Laura was plastered facefirst to the steeple. He raised his arms and grasped her around the waist, then slowly lowered her to the roof.

Carefully he turned her around, raised her chin, and studied the tears pooling in her dark eyes. His gaze dropped to her lips, and with a muttered curse he bent his head and kissed her.

Laura closed her eyes and felt a single tear roll down her cheek. Her arms encircled his neck as she stood on her toes and deepened the gentle kiss.

Josh groaned and pulled her closer. His tongue swept across her lush lower lip and begged for entrance. Desire pounded through him as her lips slowly parted, granting him his request. She pressed her body against his, her hips nudging his growing arousal.

Her fingers trembling, Laura caressed his soft black hair. Dense heat coiled in her stomach as the kiss intensified. Her breasts felt heavy, and her sensitive nipples budded against the lace of her bra. She could feel his arousal through her jeans, and was both frightened and excited by it. Josh Langley wanted her!

Josh's fingers spread across the small of her back and brought her even closer to his pleasure and pain. How could one kiss get so far out of hand? Lord, how he wanted this woman. He brought the kiss swiftly to an end. This was Laura he was kissing. This was a respectable citizen and Kelli's friend. He had no business kissing her, let alone doing what his body was crying out to do.

Her lips swollen from his kisses, Laura stared up at him. "Josh?"

He willed his heartbeat to slow down as he dragged air into his lungs. Her eyes were dark with desire and confusion. Damn, she had no right to do this to him. When she had grabbed his hand

and prevented him from falling, he'd nearly had a heart attack. She could have been crippled for life, if not killed. His voice was harsh with fear as he pulled her arms from around his neck. "If you ever pull another stunt like that, I'll throttle you."

Four

Laura's mouth formed an astonished *O* as she gazed up into Josh's angry face. What had happened? One minute he was kissing her into oblivion, the next he was threatening to throttle her. Not for a moment did she believe he would actually hit her, but he sure was upset about her lending a helping hand. He should be thanking her, she thought, not scolding her like she was a naughty child. Granted, he didn't know that Chief Snuggle Bear would never allow her to fall, but that still didn't give him the right to yell at her. He ought to be thankful that the chief allowed her to help him. The chief wasn't known for his generosity when it came to other people's problems.

With a sudden jerk Laura glanced around the darkened roof. The chief also wasn't known to allow men to kiss her. Especially the sort of intense, heated kiss she had just shared with Josh. Why hadn't he stopped it? Was it Josh, or was the chief finally going to allow her to proceed with her life?

A brilliant smile lit up her face as the door on the far side of the roof burst open. Frank, Mary, and a group of concerned citizens, all huffing and puffing from having run up three flights of stairs, piled out. Their anxious questions were shouted across the tar roof. Laura bent, picked up the hour hand, and swung it over her shoulder. A mischievous twinkle gleamed in her eye as she politely said to Josh, "You're welcome."

Josh watched her walk over to the group of people, answer a few questions, then disappear down the stairwell. He took two hurried steps after her and was jerked to a stop by the rope still tied around his waist. With a muttered curse he started to unknot the rope. Real smooth, Slick, he berated himself. First you kiss her like a rutting bull and then you threaten to thwack her. Why in the hell hadn't he thanked her for saving him from some serious injuries instead of yelling at her? He'd never raised a hand toward a woman in his life, and the only thrashing he'd ever done was when he was sixteen. An upper-class jerk had sprouted some derogatory remarks about Kelli. When he'd refused to take them back and had added a few more choice insults, Josh had given him what he seemed to be asking for. Word had spread around town as rapidly as hellfire that Josh Langley was a troublemaker and a delinquent. He never went out of his way to convince the town any differently. People had the right to their own opinions.

With a silent curse he yanked the rope from around the vent pipe and coiled it. He was dropping the wrench into his tool box when Frank joined him. "You okay, Josh?"

"Sure. It was touch-and-go there for a minute. It's a good thing Laura has a strong grip."

"Grip, hell. The way it looked from below your partner could have been Wonder Woman."

Josh snapped the toolbox closed and glanced over to the steeple. Frank was right. Laura barely reached his nose, and he outweighed her by at least sixty pounds. So how had she pulled him back up? He was distracted as Sylas, the panting bush, pushed and jabbed his way through the group. In the light of bouncing flashlights, Josh noticed the camouflage paint was running down Sylas's puffing cheeks. "Easy, Sylas. You didn't have to climb all those steps. I was coming down."

"Lord, boy, are you okay?"

"Sure. I might find a few gray hairs tomorrow, but that's all the damage that's been done." Josh gathered up his rope, toolbox, and flashlight, and herded the curious group down the steps.

Laura was sitting in the cab of the truck with the door open and dome light on, studying the list of clues. She glanced up and stared as the group pushed through the town hall's double doors. Frank and Mary were first, followed by a man tall enough to be a professional basketball player. A woman dressed in a quilted bathrobe, hair curlers, and a ragged pair of bunny slippers shuffled out next. Sylas, the human pin oak, fairly rolled down the three steps leading to the sidewalk, depositing a trail of leaves behind him. Josh, who was the last to exit, turned and locked the doors.

Laura folded the list and jammed it back into her tote bag as Josh headed around the front of the truck, casually saying good night to the departing group. He climbed in behind the wheel, closed his door, and yawned. Damn, he was tired.

Laura saw the yawn behind his hand and instantly began yawning too. "You did say we can catch some sleep after this stop, didn't you?"

Josh frowned at the exhaustion in her voice. Was he pushing her too hard. "We'll stop by your place and pick up some clean clothes for you and the items marked on the list."

"Clean clothes?"

He started the truck and chuckled as Gladys, the

woman in the bathrobe, held a conversation with a dented garbage can. "We can't separate or we'll be disqualified. Since you have only one bed and no couch, I figured we'd go to my place." As he drove away from the town hall, he wondered if she thought he was going to make a pass at her. He wouldn't blame her if she did after the kiss they had just shared. To put her mind at ease he said, "You can take the bed and I'll sleep on the couch."

Laura wondered whom he was clarifying it for, himself or her. "Sounds wonderful." She'd argue about the sleeping arrangements at his place. Right now, all she wanted was a shower.

Josh parked the truck in Laura's driveway and stared up at the town's only haunted house. The neighborhood kids were disappointed that Laura had spent two nights in the house and hadn't met Peterson's ghost yet. Rumor on the Little League team was that Peterson made his nocturnal visits to find his beloved pet schnauzer, Greta, named after his favorite actress, Greta Garbo. Poor Greta had died of a broken heart a mere two weeks after her master. The kids figured the two spirits had never found each other in heaven, so old man Peterson kept returning to the house, hoping to find her one day.

Laura climbed out of the truck and headed around back to the kitchen door. Glancing at her house, she wondered why everyone stared at it as if blood would start seeping through the walls at any moment. To her it was strong and secure, a house that had stood the test of time. It was her home. She knew it could stand a coat of light paint to brighten it up, and the front porch needed a few boards replaced. But, what the heck, it was over a hundred years old. It deserved a face-lift.

She flipped on the kitchen light and chuckled at the way Josh scanned the room, then silently headed into the living room. What was he looking for, burglars or ghosts? Pulling the list from her bag, she started to gather the items needed.

Josh finished searching the house and returned to the kitchen as Laura placed the last item into a shopping bag. "It's all clear," he said.

She raised an eyebrow as if to question his judgment. "I didn't realize burglaries were so common around here."

"They're not. It's better to be safe than sorry."

"Spoken like a true officer of the law." She watched a frown form on his brows. "Thank you, Josh. That was sweet of you to check for intruders. Why don't you help yourself to something to eat while I take a quick shower and get some clean clothes together?"

"Is there any leftover chili?"

She smiled at his hopeful expression. "In the yellow bowl behind the milk. I'll be down in a few minutes."

He had the refrigerator door open and was reaching for the yellow bowl before she even made it to the stairs.

Josh stared down at the woman sleeping on his couch. She looked younger than her twenty-eight years, with her face relaxed and her hair spread across one of his pillows. The colorful afghan his mother had crocheted was pulled up to her chin. It was a shame he had to wake her. Gently shaking her shoulder, he called, "Laura."

She mumbled something vaguely familiar and sank lower under the blanket. He chuckled and leaned closer. "Come on, sleepyhead, time to get up."

Her voice was husky as she muttered, "'The sheep's in the meadow and the cow's in the corn.'"

Josh sat down on the first thing he connected with, the coffee table. Damn, he thought. She'd solved another clue, and in her sleep no less! She was reciting the nursery rhyme about Little Boy Blue, and the "tool" used to get the cow out of the corn was a horn. How could she sleep with clues running through her head? He had tossed and turned with only one thought racing around in his mind. Laura.

After winning the argument on who slept where, she had slipped into his bathroom to change into her nightclothes. It was obvious she wasn't in the least bit concerned about spending the night with him. He wanted to remind her that just because he was a police officer didn't mean he wasn't a man. Laura was too trusting.

When she came out of his bathroom wearing a pair of baggy boxer shorts with green and pink cacti printed on them, and a fluorescent pink T-shirt large enough for a pregnant woman carrying triplets, he wondered if the outfit was supposed to be a turnoff. Because if it was, it had the opposite effect on him. He thought she looked adorable, and his imagination ran wild with visions of what she was trying to hide. She politely asked him for a pillow and placed her neatly folded clothes on the living room chair. He gave her the extra pillow from his bed and went back to the bedroom to retrieve a blanket from the top shelf of his closet. By the time he returned, she was sound asleep. He left the blanket on the coffee table and a small kitchen light burning, just in case she woke up, and headed for the shower and his bed.

It now was nine o'clock in the morning, and they both had gotten four hours sleep. Or he would have if he hadn't spent at least the first hour thinking of her. He wasn't sure if he was mad at her for sleeping so soundly while he'd stood under a cold shower, or because she'd solved another clue in her sleep. He stood up and headed for the kitchen, hoping the smell of frying bacon would wake her.

Laura woke to the aroma of coffee and bacon. She turned over on her side and slowly opened one eye. Josh was standing in the kitchen with his bare back toward her, flipping bacon. A pair of faded jeans sat low on his lean hips. What a way to wake up in the morning she thought. Seeing Josh dressed in a pair of jeans cooking breakfast was one sure way to get her blood pumping. Trying not to make a sound, she left the couch and headed for the shower.

Josh was placing two full plates on the table when she entered the kitchen. She had taken a quick shower and dressed in a comfortable pair of shorts and a sleeveless top. "Good morning, Josh. Is there anything I can do to help?"

"Nope. Sit down and eat. It's going to be another long day." He sat down opposite her and dug into his eggs, then watched in amusement as she cleaned her plate. Not many women ate like they were in training to become sumo wrestlers. "Do you lift weights?" he asked.

Surprised, she stopped in the middle of reaching for another slice of toast. "No, why?"

He took a long drink of orange juice. "Something has been bothering me. Last night you stopped me from falling off the ledge. That in itself was a mighty feat for a man, but you're a woman, and not a very big one."

Laura's eyebrows rose in confusion. Had he just insulted her or complimented her?

"The other thing that has me baffled," he went on, "is you're right-handed. Last night you held me with your left hand."

"So?"

"How would you explain your strength?"

Her eyes opened wide in pure innocence. "Adrenaline?"

He studied her guileless expression and finished his coffee. "Could be, I guess. Stranger things have happened. Right before you pulled me in, you yelled something. What was it?"

Laura flushed to the roots of her hair. How could she possibly tell him about the chief?

Intrigued by her blush, he said, "Laura?"

She lowered her gaze to the table and mumbled, "A curse."

Josh pulled the memory of that moment back into focus. It hadn't sounded like any curses he knew. He was positive that it started with a "ch" sound. "What curse?"

Laura kept her head down and played with her fork. "I'd rather not say." She quickly glanced up and saw his determined look. "I yelled it in Navaho."

"You know Navaho?"

"Only enough to fill a postcard, and that usually gets me in trouble." No truer words were ever spoken. She knew only a handful of phrases and the ancient chant to call up a guardian spirit. With all the trouble those few words had brought her, there was no way she was learning another word of Navaho.

Josh read the embarrassment in her eyes and tactfully changed the subject. "Do you know you talk in your sleep?"

"I do?"

"You also solved another clue. When I tried to wake you earlier, you started reciting a nursery rhyme. 'Little boy blue, come blow your horn. The sheep's in the meadow, the cow's in the corn.'"

She grinned. "That means only sixty-eight to go."

Josh cleaned off the table except for the coffee cups while Laura grabbed her tote bag filled with books. "Plus, we still have to find six items that we know of," she added.

As she slipped on her glasses, Josh disappeared into the bedroom. She hoped he was going to finish dressing. It was too difficult to concentrate with his gleaming muscular chest sitting four feet away. She glanced up when he came back to the table fully dressed and hid her sigh of relief. "Does the barbershop on Main Street have one of those poles?" she asked. "The kind that spins around and is red and white?"

"Yes. It's connected next to the door. Why?"

"Then I just solved another one. 'Round and round it goes, red over white, red over white.'"

Josh nodded. "The tricky part about getting it will be convincing Ed to turn the electricity off long enough for me to disconnect it."

"Do you think you can?"

"I'll try. Last year scavenger hunters took both of his barber chairs Friday night and Ed couldn't do any business all day Saturday. At least this year he can still cut hair."

Laura finished her coffee and glanced up at the clock. It was almost ten. "I vote we gather up the items we need this morning, and over lunch we can work on some more clues."

"Sounds good to me. First stop will be Ed's barbershop." Josh dumped the rest of the dishes into the sink while Laura jammed books back into her tote. She picked up the list, her pocketbook, and tote, and headed for the door.

Josh caught up with her at the bottom of the stairs. They entered the garage and walked over to the truck. Josh paused with his hand on the handle of her door.

Laura saw his hesitation and raised a questioning eyebrow.

He cleared his throat. "I never thanked you properly for pulling me back up onto the ledge."

She noticed his serious expression and wondered if she was in for another lecture. "You're welcome."

He moved in front of her, forcing her to back up against the truck. "You know I wouldn't have throttled you. I just said that because I was scared."

She tilted her head up. "Of falling?"

"No." With a finger he gently pushed back a wisp of hair that had escaped her ponytail. "I was scared of you falling."

She leaned against the truck, unsure if her legs would support her weight. "I wasn't going to fall," she said, her voice soft with awe and understanding. She felt Josh's gaze bore into her. How could she clarify it more? Her teeth worried her lower lip.

Josh's finger shook as he tenderly forced her lip away from her teeth. "Don't," he pleaded. "Every time you do that, your lip becomes moist and swollen, and I go out of my mind thinking of kissing you."

She felt the heat of his gaze down to her toes. Thank you, Lord, she prayed silently. He was going to kiss her again. She watched, hypnotized, as his eyes darkened and he lowered his head toward hers.

Josh stopped his descent a mere breath away from her waiting lips. "Thank you, Laura," he whispered, and captured her mouth in a sweet, gentle kiss.

Disappointment shot through her as Josh broke the kiss. If you could call it a kiss. She'd been kissed with more passion in the eighth grade. What had happened to the heat? Bewildered, she glanced around the garage, looking for the only reason that made sense. Chief Snuggle Bear. He had to be behind this somehow.

"Come on, partner," Josh said briskly. "Time's a wasting."

He held her door open while she climbed in. After closing the door, he walked around the back of the truck and took a deep breath. Lord, that was close. He had struggled against the unquenchable desire to savor her kisses and had instead placed a chaste peck on her welcoming lips. If he had kissed her the way his body was screaming for him to, they would not have left the garage anytime within the near future. Say a week or two.

He got into the truck, started the engine, and hit the electronic garage door opener. "Okay, partner, I'm open to any suggestions you might have on how to win this hunt."

Laura was staring out the side window wondering what the chief had done to Josh. She knew he'd been about to kiss her until her hair either went completely curly or perfectly straight. That kiss had been in his eyes and on his lips. She had known it. She had felt it. So why hadn't she gotten it?

A silent sigh escaped her lips at Josh's words. He was playing it safe. "The schedule isn't working?" she asked as he turned onto Main and pulled into a parking space.

"Hardly. We were off it within the first two hours."

She chuckled at the disgust in his voice. She could have told him a schedule wouldn't work, they never do. Babies never stick to a schedule, and airlines are either ahead of or behind schedule. Doctors' appointment books with all their "scheduled" appointments every fifteen minutes were a laugh. Every time she went to one, she considered herself lucky if she actually saw the doctor on the same day as the "scheduled appointment."

Life was not something you could schedule. You

just lived it. She slid from the truck and followed him to the turning barber pole. "You go in and sweet-talk Ed while I guard it."

Josh placed the toolbox on the sidewalk and groaned. "You obviously haven't met Ed yet."

Laura grinned as Josh opened the door. A bell tinkled, and he disappeared inside. Curious, she moved over and peeked inside the shop. Nostalgia swept over her; it was like turning on *The Andy Griffith Show*. Two old gentlemen were playing checkers in the back, and one even looked like Floyd. Her smile faded as a huge giant of a man lumbered out of the back room. He was dressed in a white smock, black cossack pants, and combat boots. This was Ed? He stood six foot six, weighed about two hundred and eighty pounds, and looked like he belonged on *Wrestlemania*. He was blocking the way to his two red leather barber chairs, and was quietly arguing with Josh.

She watched as Josh cheerfully explained he hadn't come for a chair. Ed raised his bushy black brows. Josh must have told him what he was after, because he pointed to the pole. Laura gasped as Ed went deathly white, clutched his chest, and violently shook his head. Josh pulled out the list and showed it to Ed. She worried her lower lip while Josh and Ed argued back and forth. After what seemed like hours, Josh came out grinning.

"You got it?" she asked.

He took one look at her lower lip and sighed. "I told you not to do that." He regretfully shook his head and placed a light kiss on her surprised mouth. Standing back, he admired the flush staining her cheeks. "Ed went in the back to turn off the electricity so I can disconnect the pole."

Laura laughed at his little-boy smile of victory. "Why didn't you tell me Ed was enormous? For a minute there I thought you were a dead man."

"So did I. Ed is as peaceful as a lamb, and

normally would give you the shirt off his back, except when it comes to his shop. He wasn't very happy when someone borrowed his chairs last year, but we explained this was an American custom. His chairs were the first items to be put back and installed to his satisfaction."

A shudder slid down her spine as she envisioned Ed's reaction to someone stealing his beloved chairs. "How did you convince him to let you have his pole?"

"I showed him the list and he agreed it looked like the clue for a barber pole. So I explained that if I took it down, he could watch and make sure I did it right."

Laura's eyes widened as Ed came outside. He was bigger than she had thought. "Ed," Josh said, "I would like you to meet my partner, Laura Bryant. She just moved into the old Peterson place and will be working at *The Union Station Review*."

Ed's voice rolled like black thunder as he shook her hand. "It's a pleasure to make your acquaintance."

She was amazed at the gentleness of his touch. "Thank you, Ed."

He smiled down at her and released her hand, then quickly turned and glared at Josh. "She stays alone in the Halloween House?"

Josh's mouth went dry as he met Ed's hostile stare. Was it his fault she had purchased a haunted house? He hadn't even been in town when she'd visited, gotten a job, and bought the Peterson place.

Laura laid a hand on Ed's arm. "Josh has nothing to do with where I live, Ed."

"He's your partner, *da*?"

"Yes, but only for the scavenger hunt. The house is mine and I like it very much."

"No spooks?" To make sure he was using the

proper word, Ed spread his arms wide and moaned, "Ooooooo."

Laura bit the inside of her cheek to keep from laughing at the picture he made, moaning and flapping his arms. She was tempted to tell him that one lived on her third floor, but she had brought it with her. "No ghosts, goblins, banshees, or spooks."

Ed looked unconvinced. "When you see one, you call Ed, *da?*"

"If a spook bothers me, I'll call you."

A look that said *it's settled* appeared on Ed's craggy face. "Josh, you take down pole now and be careful. Laura Bryant, you come inside, I show photographs of my boys." With a meaningful glance at Josh, he added, "They are not afraid of spooks."

Josh watched as Ed and Laura disappeared into the shop. What did Ed mean by that crack about his boys not being afraid? He wasn't scared of ghosts. They didn't exist. If Laura did happen upon a spook though, she'd better call him, or the police. Since he was the police, Josh figured he had all the bases covered. Rescuing damsels who looked like Laura could have some great benefits.

Laura pushed away her empty plate and glared at Josh. "I'm telling you, *Miami Vice* opened with a shot of flamingos."

"Wrong, it opened with bikinis. Polka-dotted bikinis, to be precise." Josh reached for the bag of potato chips.

"For a cop, you sure aren't observant." She sighed as Josh grinned wolfishly. "Okay, partner, what do we do now?"

"Get both items. Do you own a bikini? Because I know where we can find a flamingo."

Laura pushed back her chair and headed upstairs. "One bikini coming up."

Josh glanced at Laura's kitchen clock and groaned. Three o'clock in the afternoon. That left just fifteen hours and they had only thirty-seven items, counting the flamingo/bikini. How was he ever going to earn the town's respect if he couldn't decipher these clues? With renewed determination, he grabbed the first page of the list and started going through it again.

A minute later Laura dropped a cloth bag on the table, sat down, and picked up the list where she had left off. Josh looked up from his page and glanced at the bag. He read the same clue again, then looked back at the bag. It was an awfully small bag. He reread the clue for the third time and peeked at the bag. The bag wasn't just small, it was itsy-bitsy. There was no way she could have an entire bathing suit in that miniature bag. "Laura, I think we need both pieces of the suit."

She glanced up from the thesaurus and pushed her glasses back up her nose. "Both pieces are in the bag."

Josh felt the sweat break out across his forehead. Lord, have mercy, he thought. Laura wore what was in that microscopic bag to lie out in the sun. She must use a lot of suntan lotion! He avoided looking at the bag again and reached for his glass of iced tea.

"Stop the truck!" Laura cried.

Josh slammed on the brakes and grabbed for the pile of books sliding off the seat. "What's wrong?"

"Nothing's wrong. Just back the truck up slowly and quietly."

He muttered something undecipherable and jammed the truck into reverse. At least this time he hadn't run over anything. She'd probably seen a petunia sprout legs and waltz down the street.

"There, look!"

Josh stopped and looked to where her finger was pointing. In his amazement, his foot slipped off the brake pedal, causing them to drift backward. Laura's warning saved him from knocking over a cluster of empty garbage cans.

Laura turned and looked out the back window in time to see one of the trash cans get up and walk a few feet away. When it found a fresh patch of grass with a view of the surrounding street and houses, it gingerly lowered itself back down. In a reprimanding tone, she said, "You almost smashed Harley."

"Forget Harley. Did you see everything Frank and Mary were carrying?"

"Was that Frank and Mary? I didn't recognize them with the canoe on their heads."

"Mary's orange high-top sneakers and fuchsia bermuda shorts were the giveaway. Now, tell me what you saw?"

"First there was the canoe, and then the funny-looking dog."

Josh glanced up from the dictionary, where he was furiously writing in the margins. "That wasn't a dog, Laura. It was a goat."

"Are you sure?"

"Yes, I'm sure. I know a goat when I see one."

"So would I," she snapped. "I say it was a funny-looking dog."

"You didn't have your glasses on, and they were fifty yards away. It was a goat."

She crossed her arms over her chest and glared at him. "Are you making fun of my glasses?"

"No," he whispered as he unsnapped his seat belt and slid over to her. "I think your glasses are adorable." He gently pushed back a stray lock of sun-streaked hair. "Do you know your eyes mirror your feelings? I can tell what you're thinking just by looking into you eyes."

Laura nervously ran her tongue over her lips. She was in some serious trouble if he really could tell what she was thinking. Right at this moment, she wanted him to kiss her as he had on the roof the previous night. She wanted the moist fire to flow between her thighs and her blood to heat. She wanted to feel like a woman and to know a man's touch. Her gaze locked helplessly with his while she prayed and feared he could read her every thought.

Josh's body responded instantly to the desire shimmering in the depths of her eyes. His breathing grew ragged, his chest tightened, and every ounce of spare blood rushed to his groin. He wanted this woman. With a trembling finger he reached out and followed the wet path her tongue left. Her lips felt feverish beneath his touch. Would she feel as hot lying naked beneath him?

He was lowering his mouth to taste her heat when a sudden movement caught his attention. Turning his head, he watched as a dented trash can strolled out into the middle of the street. His groan of frustration was muffled against his clenched fist as a deep-echoing voice emerged from the can. "Are you two all right?"

Laura blinked twice and gawked at the silver can. No, she wasn't all right. She was about to rip the police chief's shirt off and take the law into her own hands. What in the heck was she doing?

Josh cleared his throat. "We're fine, Harley. I hope I didn't scare you too badly."

"After having the Wilsons' Doberman try to knock me over all morning, your back bumper looked like a picnic."

Laura found her voice and managed a shaky "Hi, Harley."

The garbage can did a fair imitation of a bow.

"Hello, pretty lady. You must be Laura, who's been saying hello to me."

A flush swept up her cheeks. Now it seemed crazy that every time she had passed a trash can, she'd knocked on it and whispered hello to Harley. "How many times did I actually get the right can?"

"Four, and let me thank you for brightening up my night." Harley turned and started down the street.

"You're welcome," Laura called as the waddling can rounded the corner and disappeared from sight.

Josh returned to his side of the seat and fastened the safety belt. Nothing like a conversation with a garbage can to break the mood, he thought dryly. He should be thankful that Harley happened along. Imagine getting caught necking in the front seat of his father's borrowed pickup truck in broad daylight. He was thirty years old, not some horny sixteen-year-old sophomore.

Laura glanced at Josh. He looked dangerous. Was he upset because Harley had interrupted, or because for one wild moment he had wanted her? Didn't she meet his standards? What was wrong with her? She had a decent job, owned her own home, and came complete with her very own guardian spirit. Her face was passable, her body could inspire construction workers to whistle, and her teeth were all her own. What more could a man want?

A sigh caught in her throat. Maybe it was a good thing Josh hadn't touched her. There was no telling what Chief Snuggle Bear would have done. She was beginning to like this town and Josh's friendship. There was no sense in jeopardizing them both by bringing the chief's wrath upon them.

Josh heard her sigh and gritted his teeth. He

released the emergency brake and dropped the shifter into gear. With meticulous care he drove up the street and forced his grip to relax on the steering wheel. "What else did you see Frank and Mary carrying?"

Five

"Josh!" Laura whispered. "Something's sniffing my ankle!"

Holding in the air the bucket he was using to empty the water trough, Josh peered through the darkness at the small shape near Laura's leg. "It's only one of the piglets. Whatever you do, don't step on it."

Laura kept the flashlight focused on the water trough as she bent down and petted the baby pig. "Hello, boy, did we wake you?" The piglet squealed and butted its head against her palm. "Look, Josh, he likes me."

Josh tilted the trough and scooped up the last of the water. "That's nice." He set down the empty trough and bucket. "Be careful with that little fellow, he's worth his weight in gold."

With a final pat and a gentle push, Laura tried sending him back over to his mama and the other sleeping piglets. She chuckled when he squealed and rubbed his snout against her sneaker.

"I can manage the trough by myself," Josh said. "You take the bucket and the flashlights." He hoisted the metal container and headed for the gate. He was halfway through the opening when the barrel of a shotgun stopped him.

"Take another step and it will be your last."

"Charlie, for Pete's sake," Josh exclaimed. "Put that gun down before you hurt someone."

"Josh?"

"If you had turned on some outside lights, you could see it was me." Josh felt the double barrel press against his chest and swallowed hard. Charlie McPhearson was known to be a little eccentric when it came to Annabelle, his prize Spotted Swine. In a protective gesture he pulled Laura behind him. "We didn't hurt Annabelle or the piglets. We came only for the water trough."

"Who's that behind you?"

Laura closed her eyes and prayed Charlie wouldn't shoot her or Josh for trespassing. She didn't want to die. She especially didn't want to die in a pigpen. Where in the hell was the chief? For the past ten years he'd been breathing over her shoulder watching her every move, and now that she needed him, he was nowhere around. She took a step closer to Josh and pressed against his back.

In an authoritative voice Josh snapped, "Charlie, put down the gun. You're scaring Laura." Who in the hell was he kidding? He was scared spitless himself that Charlie's finger would slip and he'd end up killing both Laura and him with one bullet.

Josh breathed a sigh of relief as the gun slowly lowered to point at the ground. "Thank you. Charlie McPhearson, I would like to introduce you to my scavenger hunt partner, Laura Bryant. She moved into town a couple of days ago and will be working at *The Union Station Review*."

Charlie peered at the dark silhouette that detached itself from Josh. "Is this part of the scavenger hunt?" he asked.

"Yes," Josh said. "Annabelle's water trough was one of the items. We just figured it out, and since it's two-thirty in the morning, I didn't think you'd appreciate us knocking on your door to ask permission. I already wrote you a note and pinned it on your front door, explaining that I'd taken the trough and would return it as soon as the judging was done tomorrow."

"You were going to leave Annabelle without any water?" Charlie asked incredulously.

"I was going to leave the bucket full, but I was worried something could knock it over and hurt one of her piglets. So I thought it would be better not to leave anything. I know you get up at four-thirty every morning and would take care of Annabelle."

Charlie thought it over, then nodded his head in agreement. "How do you know the water trough's one of the items?"

Josh repeated the clue, word by word. "'Salon for the grunting knighthood that exist in a pen.'"

"How did you get Annabelle's trough out of that?"

Laura found her voice. "As soon as we figured that pigs grunt and live in a pen, Josh knew it had to be Annabelle." She glanced over and saw moonlight gleaming off the shotgun. For added insurance she gushed, "She's considered royalty around these parts."

Charlie's chest puffed with pride. His Annabelle and her babies had been called knighthood. He liked that. "Okay, you can take the trough on one condition."

Josh glanced at Laura and shrugged. "What's that?"

"I was going to name the piglets after some of my wife's relatives, but you changed my mind. I need eight names of knights. You know, the ones from the Round Table."

"You mean King Arthur and the Knights of the Round Table?" Laura asked.

"Arthur?" After a moment of silence Charlie said, "I like that. It has a nice ring to it. Name seven more."

"Sir Lancelot," Josh said.

"Are there any girl piglets?" Laura asked.

"Two."

"Queen Guinevere and Morgan le Fay."

"That's four," Charlie said.

Laura dug through her memory and could only come up with one more. "Sir Gawain."

Josh drew a complete blank at naming another knight. "How about Merlin? He was King Arthur's wizard."

Charlie chuckled. "Yeah, that would do. One piglet looks kind of brainy."

Laura stared down at the baby pig trying to eat her shoelace and wondered how a pig looked intelligent. "You could name one Camelot."

"Wasn't that the town King Arthur lived in?" Charlie asked.

"It was his kingdom," Josh said.

"Yeah, Camelot sounds better than Mildred any day. One more and you got yourselves a water trough until tomorrow afternoon."

Josh looked over at Laura. A spark flashed in his eyes the same instant her head snapped up. In perfect unison they said, "Excalibur."

"Isn't that a car?"

"They named the car after King Arthur's sword, Excalibur."

"Wow, they are some pretty fancy names for hogs," Charlie said.

"From what I hear," Laura said sincerely, "they are some pretty fancy hogs."

"You got that right, little lady." Pride vibrated in his voice as he straightened his shoulders and repeated, "You got that right."

In the darkened barnyard Josh hurried Laura through the gate and secured it behind them.

"Thanks for the use of the trough, Charlie. We'll return it as soon as we can."

"No need. I'll be in town tomorrow to see who wins. I'll pick it up from you then. Nice meeting you, Laura."

"The pleasure was mine, Mr. McPhearson," she called as she hurried down the driveway after Josh.

Laura grabbed the dashboard with one hand and the armrest with the other as Josh turned off the highway onto a dirt road. She cast a quick glance at the silent man beside her. He hadn't spoken a word since leaving the McPhearson place. The left front tire struck a rut in the road, and the bone-jarring bounce knocked her pile of books off the seat. They had been using the cab of the pickup as an on-the-road office since the hunt began. It was now littered with books, papers, empty paper cups, and candy wrappers.

Her eyes followed the twin beams of the headlights as Josh expertly maneuvered the truck around ruts, gullies, and overgrown branches. "Where are we going?"

He didn't answer, only tightened his hands on the wheel as he maneuvered the truck around a curve. A cloud of dust rose as he slammed on the brake and turned off the engine. He undid his seat belt and turned to face her.

She undid her belt and faced him. The interior of the truck was pitch-black and she could hardly make out his features. She'd glimpsed an old deserted house in the distance before Josh had turned out the headlights. They were in the middle of nowhere. The distant sounds of frogs and peepers gave testimony to a pond being nearby.

The last two items they'd deciphered were a box

of Quaker Oats and teeth. "I don't think we'll find any cereal here," she said hesitantly.

His voice was low and intense as it streaked through the darkness. "I don't give a damn about the hunt."

Laura shuddered at the controlled violence in his tone. What was he upset about? She clasped her trembling hands together and whispered in confusion, "I don't understand."

His hand shook as he reached across the seat and pulled her to him. "Don't you realize how close you came to being shot?"

Her palms absently caressed his chest as she gazed up at him. What was he talking about? she wondered. The shotgun hadn't been pointed at her. And who cared what his mouth was saying? The pounding of his heart was telling her something different. Her hands slowly rose and feathered across the open collar of his shirt. She could feel the rhythm of his heart and the quickness of his breath. He had to care something about her if he was upset that she could have been shot. With renewed confidence she prayed that Chief Snuggle Bear would stay wherever he was, then leaned into Josh's embrace. In a husky whisper she said, "Kiss me."

Josh's heart slammed against his chest at the sound of her sweet words. He shouldn't kiss her, but damn, they both could have been shot by Charlie. A raw groan of need ripped from his throat as he bent and took her lips.

Heat. Moist, delirious heat softened her body as she melted against him. Her breathing was ragged as he broke the kiss and trailed a path of fire down her arched throat. Her fingers clenched in his hair as she propelled his lips back up. She needed his mouth.

She moaned in ecstasy as her lips sealed over his. When his teeth lightly nipped at her lower lip, she nipped back, then ran her tongue over the area. Josh shuddered and she smiled against his demanding mouth.

Josh felt her smile and deepened the kiss. His tongue boldly explored the sweetness of her mouth. Her breasts pressed into his chest as she shifted her weight and brought one jean-clad thigh over his leg.

Laura bumped the steering wheel with her hip and shifted her weight again. This time she settled more fully against Josh's arousal. She felt the heat of his hands through her cotton blouse and imagined what they would feel like stroking her skin. She dragged in desperately needed air as Josh rained kisses across her cheek and tenderly tugged on her earlobe with his teeth.

This felt so right. She was in heaven in his arms with the devil dancing in her head. She wanted Josh Langley in her bed. She wanted him naked, hard, and hot. Half of her was embarrassed by her wanton desires, while the other half was excited. She might technically be a virgin, but she knew and understood the human body. Both male and female.

She threw back her head, offering her neck to his mouth. He strung a line of kisses down her satiny skin and playfully bit the top button of her blouse. He tried to control the slight tremor in his hands as he spanned her waist, then slowly raised his hands up to cup her breasts.

His name escaped her parted lips as she closed her eyes and reveled in the sensations invading her body. Her breath caught as his thumbs flipped over her hardened nipples.

Josh closed his eyes in pleasure, then immediately opened them to flashing blue and red lights. *The cops!* In a blinding flash of panic and embarrassment, he shoved Laura away and muttered a curse.

Laura's eyes flew open to see what the chief had done this time. She expected to see giant mutant killer frogs attacking the truck, or a ten-foot-long rattlesnake curled up on the hood. What she saw was a patrol car parked behind them very politely flashing its lights in warning.

She glanced at Josh sitting in the glare of red and blue lights. Disappointment and happiness flared through her at the same time. She was frustrated to be stopped when things were starting to get interesting, but she was ecstatic to know the chief had nothing to do with it. Was he finally going to let her lead her own life, or was the permission granted due to Josh?

The patrol car must belong to Cal, Josh's deputy, she thought. A small chuckle started in the back of her throat and grew into a full-blown laugh before she could control it. The sheriff has been caught necking in a parked truck by his own deputy.

Josh glared into the rearview mirror at Cal, then turned his scowl on the woman sitting beside him, laughing. He didn't need this. He was dead tired, hungry, and aroused. For one split second, when he first saw the flashing lights, he'd reverted back to his teenage years, when the cops were always trying to pin something on him. His instinct was to push away anyone close to him, so he could face the police alone.

He gave a silent prayer of thanks for the lights discoloring the interior of the truck. Laura surely could not see the bright flood of red seeping into his cheeks. His toes were embarrassed, his knees mortified, and other body parts would have been humiliated if they weren't so rigid. With a muttered curse directed to his deputy, who just might not be his deputy much longer, he got out of the truck and slammed the door. While slowly walking toward the patrol car, he promised himself that one day he would laugh at this. It might be a long time coming, but one day he would see some humor.

"Please, Josh, can't we just go to bed?" Laura pleaded.

Josh stopped in mid-stride and stared at the bent head of the woman he was pulling across his grandparents' backyard. His brain knew she meant to sleep, but his body was preparing itself for the other meaning. Lord, he was tired, and Laura was asleep on her feet. "I promise within ten minutes you will be tucked in bed. This is our last stop. I would love to have left you sleeping in the truck, but we can't chance being caught separated."

Laura blinked the sleep from her eyes and gently shook her head. Even as she sank farther into the warmth of Josh's windbreaker, she forced herself awake. How many hours had it been since she'd slept. A little voice in the back of her mind said, The same amount as Josh, and you don't see him walking around like a zombie.

"Okay, I'm awake," she mumbled. She stared at the back of his grandparents' house and asked, "What are we getting here?"

Josh pulled her along to the back door, inserted his key, and unlocked it. "The last item." Without turning on the lights, he took her hand and gently pushed her into a soft chair. "Don't move and don't make a sound," he whispered into her ear, then disappeared into the darkness.

Laura curled up in the chair and sighed. Her eyes drifted closed as she tried to remember what the last item was. When Josh had returned to the truck after talking with Cal, they had pulled back onto the highway and headed for the diner. She remembered using the back door that led directly into the kitchen and meeting the cook.

room. She had used Josh's shower and blow dryer. It felt great to be clean and awake.

Josh smiled as she sailed into the kitchen, bringing the sun with her. She was dressed in red, royal blue, and gold plaid shorts, with a sleeveless gold top, white sneakers, and gold socks. Her hair was pulled up high into a saucy ponytail, a pair of gold-rimmed sunglasses were perched on top of her head, and dangling golden lightning bolts hung from her ears. Her face was bare of makeup and her generous mouth answered his smile.

"Well, partner, do you think we won?" she asked.

"Good morning to you too."

Laura reached for the coffee cup he was holding out to her. "Thanks, and good morning." She sat down and poured a river of syrup over the pancakes stacked on her plate. "Why didn't you put me on the couch? You could have taken the bed. Better yet, you should have woken me up so I could have gotten undressed."

Josh concentrated on cutting his pancakes into neat little squares. He did not want to think about Laura getting undressed. "I didn't think you'd appreciate me taking off your clothes."

She swallowed her first mouthful of the delicious pancakes and muttered, "It would have been better than sleeping with my bra wrapped around my neck."

His fingers shook as he dropped his fork and pushed back his chair. "I'll take my shower now.

Laura's mouth fell open as he strode from the room. With a bemused shake of her head she picked up his full plate and placed it in the microwave. It was only eleven o'clock. They had a full hour before they were due at the judging stand.

Josh placed a small box on the front seat of the truck and backed out of the garage. Laura glanced at the box with dawning horror. The last item was a set of teeth. "Joshua Franklin Langley, you stole your grandmother's teeth!"

"Do I look like the kind of grandson who would steal his grandmother's dentures?"

She cringed at his tone of injustice. Maybe she was a little hasty in judging him. "I'm sorry, Josh. What's in the box?"

He turned the truck onto Main Street and parked in their designated area. He opened his door, then glanced back at her, grinning devilishly. "My grandfather's dentures."

Laura slammed her door shut and hurried after him to the judging stand. "You're despicable. How could you?"

He grabbed her hand and pulled her along. They signed in with two minutes to spare and walked back to the truck. "There are my grandparents now," he said, "sitting next to my parents. Does Gramps look upset to you?"

She glanced over to where he was pointing. Ida Langley and her husband had matching lawn chairs and were proudly sitting in the front row. The man, who was an older version of Josh, and the nice-looking woman beside them waved. Laura raised her hand and waved back. Ida smiled, while Gramps did a funny grimace that could be mistaken for a smile, and saluted Josh.

"He doesn't seem too upset," Laura admitted. "But that doesn't excuse you. The poor man couldn't eat breakfast this morning."

"Grams probably fixed him oatmeal or something."

Laura leaned against the side of the truck and watched the last team sign in. "Just make sure you give him his teeth back before lunch."

Laura estimated at least two hundred people had set up folding chairs in the park to watch the judging. Josh had explained that the judges would read each clue and name the item. The hunters were to take the correct item out of their vehicles and place it on the street directly in front of them. The team with the most correct items won. If all the items Josh and Laura had collected were right, they would have a total of fifty-two. Was it good enough to win?

The head judge announced it was twelve o'clock and the counting would commence. Out of the thirty-seven teams entered, only thirty-two teams had qualified for the prizes. As the judge announced each team, a cheer went up from the crowd in the park. Josh dragged Laura out from between their truck and the one next to them as their names were announced. She prayed no one would notice the blush staining her cheeks.

Josh took off the tarp while she pulled out their list. The first two items they did not have. As the afternoon sun beat down, the piles in front of the assorted vehicles grew. With an anxious eye she and Josh tried to determine who had the most items. A wild cheer went up when the clue for the hour hand on the town clock was read and Josh proudly placed it by their pile.

Laura glanced down to where Frank and Mary stood laughing with their pitifully small pile. The goat, or strange-looking dog, was eating a dogwood tree they had dug up somewhere and added to the mountain of stuff spilling over from their loaded-down truck.

An elderly couple dressed in their Sunday best were by their '55 Plymouth, calmly maneuvering a tombstone over to their pile. Laura bit back a chuckle as two farmers tilted their hats at the couple and easily lifted the marker onto the pile.

Josh eyed Laura as she watched the other contestants. She sparkled. When someone figured out a clue they hadn't, she clapped the hardest and shouted her congratulations. He stopped counting what the other teams had. It didn't matter any-more if he won or lost. He'd found something more important in this scavenger hunt than tomb-stones and birdbaths. He'd found Laura.

When the announcer said they were looking for pink flamingos that opened the *Miami Vice* televi-sion series, Laura whooped and pulled the plastic bird from the bed of the truck. She childishly stuck out her tongue at Josh and proudly placed the bird on their pile.

By the time the announcer read the ninetieth clue, Laura was biting her fingernails. They had to win, she thought. It meant so much to Josh. He deserved to win. He was the one who'd had a shotgun pointed at him. He was the one who'd sunk low enough to steal his grandfather's den-tures and to take a stuffed Snoopy from a toddler. It wasn't important that his grandfather was shouting encouragements to them behind a tooth-less grin, or that one of the Camerons' youngsters was happily wearing Josh's badge. What was im-portant was that he won and showed the town what a brilliant sheriff he was.

"Before we read the ninety-sixth clue," the judge said, breaking into Laura's thoughts, "we have a special announcement to make."

The crowd quieted and the contestants all turned toward the stand. Laura felt Josh grab her hand and squeeze. "By our latest tallies," the judge continued, "there is a three-way tie for first place."

Wild cheers and pandemonium broke out in the park. Money suddenly appeared as the towns-people placed their bets on the team they felt would win. The high school band struck up a lively number as the announcer tried to quiet everyone.

Laura watched as Josh communicated silently with Logan across the park, using hand signals.

Josh grinned and turned to her. "How many of the last five items do we have?"

She checked the list, then glanced in the back of the truck. "Four. Why?"

"Logan, my father, and Gramps have been keeping score. They figure the race is tied between the Paulys, the Kowalski brothers, and us."

She glanced back down at the list. "Is having four good?"

"That all depends on what they have."

Laura sighed and reread the one hundredth clue. "David could have used one instead." It still made no sense. She applauded the other contestants as they placed their items on the piles, but she kept count on what the minister and his wife, and the Kowalski brothers, found.

Josh held her hand and pulled her closer as the announcer got ready to read the one hundredth clue. "If the Paulys and the Kowalski brothers have this," he said, "it's a three-way tie. If they don't, we got it."

The announcer cleared his throat. "The clue reads, 'David could have used one instead.' The clue refers to David and Goliath. As you know, David used a slingshot. The item we are looking for is a brassiere."

Catcalls and whistles broke the air as the first team held up a brassiere that had to be a 48C. Josh moved away from Laura to get a better look at some of the finer women's garments being held up for display. Jokes were flying back and forth as to who the owners were.

Laughter erupted as Mrs. Plume, a fiesty woman in her eighties, stood up and demanded the Kowalski brothers return her brassiere.

Josh was so busy enjoying the show, he failed to notice Laura sinking back deeper between the trucks. She glanced around nervously and unclasped the front hook on her bra. She pulled one strap down over her arm, then the other, then yanked the bra through the armhole of her sweater.

She moved back up in time to see the Paulys wave a white cotton brassiere and place it in their pile. She and Josh were going to win with her bra.

The announcer spoke Josh's name. He was getting ready to shake his head when Laura thrust something in his hand and shoved him out into the street.

Bewildered, he raised his hand. There, dangling from his fingers, was a scrap of peach lace and satin that could have made a French streetwalker blush.

Six

Josh swallowed hard and fought the blush creeping up his neck as the population of Union Station went speechless. Within a heartbeat the park went wild with male cheers of approval. Josh gingerly placed the bra on their pile and stepped back toward the truck and Laura. His face was expressionless as he watched the remaining contestants wave their brassieres.

Laura folded her arms across her chest as the announcer banged on the table with a gavel. "May I have your attention. We have a winner. The winning team is Josh Langley and Laura Bryant by a bra—" he wiped at his feverish brow. "I mean, by an item."

Shouts of victory and groans of defeat accompanied the flash of money exchanging hands as Laura and Josh made their way up to the judge's stand. Laura laughed and waved to the crowd when the mayor of Union Station handed her the winning certificates. Josh felt as if his face were cracking from the smile he had plastered on it. He accepted his certificate with a nod and a murmured, "Thanks."

As they headed back to their pile, Laura suppressed a gasp as Josh grabbed her hand. He fairly dragged her across the street into the sheriff's office. She glanced around at the two empty desks and curiously looked into the vacant cell.

Josh watched as Laura waltzed around his office and started to read the wanted posters on the bulletin-board. Didn't she realize how disturbed he was that she'd whipped off her bra in the middle of the judging? Lord sakes, every man in town now knew what kind of brassiere she wore! The Kowalski brothers had drooled, the mayor had stammered, and his own grandfather had laughed and stomped his feet in approval. She couldn't be that naive as to not know what kind of speculation was going about how he had gotten the bra.

He leaned against the door, crossed his arms, and demanded, "Why in the hell did you do it?"

Laura jumped at his angry tone. She knew he was upset about the bra business, but what right did he have to yell at her as if he had caught her soliciting sailors on Main Street? One of her eyebrows arched as she stated the obvious. "To win."

"We were tied for first place," he said, exasperated.

"It's not the same." She strode to the middle of the room and faced him squarely. "Is it illegal to remove an article of clothing during the judging?"

"No, whatever we came with could be used in competition." He pushed away from the door and pulled the bit of peach lace from his shorts pocket, where he had jammed it after they were announced the winners. Somehow it had seemed indecent to leave her bra lying on top of the birdbath. "Obviously you came wearing this."

She snatched the bra from his hand. "I would think every woman there had one on. What's the big deal?"

"The big deal is you took yours off!" he shouted.

"To win!" she shouted back. She stomped over to

the first door she saw, threw it open, and entered. A string hit her in the face. Muttering a curse, she reached up and yanked. A light turned on. Great, she was in a closet.

She wrenched her sweater off over her head and tossed it down next to a bulletproof vest and assorted riot gear. She put the bra on, then slipped her top back over her head. As she opened the door, she yanked the light off.

Josh took a calming breath as she stormed out of the closet. Laura was new in town and didn't realize the gossip her actions could cause. If he hadn't threatened Cal last night with crossing-guard duty for a year, the rumors would already be spreading. For the past four years he had walked the straight and narrow line, not giving the town one piece of gossip. Now, unknowingly, Laura had provided the spark that could rekindle the fire.

Ever since he was a long-haired sixteen-year-old, the town's opinion of him could be summed up in one word. Trouble. Fathers forbade their daughters to speak to him while the local cops harassed him just for breathing. If someone pulled the fire alarm in school, they came looking for him. If someone spray-painted curse words on town hall, he was declared guilty. Out of angry pride, he never defended himself. Then, the spring of his senior year, Julie Burke, the pampered daughter of the richest man in town, found herself pregnant and pointed the finger at him. He heatedly denied the accusation.

Julie's condition increased along with the town's contempt for a young man who would not "do his duty." The only people who stood beside him other than his parents and grandparents were Kelli and her foster father, Ben. The week before the senior prom, Julie, who'd been denied the honor of being crowned prom queen because of her pregnancy, broke down and announced the truth. Dale Hamil,

the boys' high school gym teacher, had the dubi-
ous honor of tainting the Burkes' blue blood. Julie
was slipped out of town, Dale Hamil was dismissed
and never heard from again, and the God-fearing
citizens of Union Station avoided the angry young
man who had been wrongly accused.

Josh grabbed his diploma, rode out of town with
his head held high, and took the first steps toward
his chosen career. He earned a bachelor's degree in
criminology in three years, attended the police
academy, and spent his first four years as a policeman doing foot patrol in Philadelphia.

He had returned to Union Station clean-shaven
and mature enough not to listen to any gossip.
Until now. It hurt knowing he could be the cause of
Laura's name being dragged through the mud. His
voice was sad and his eyes were serious as he
asked, "Don't you realize the whole town will be
wondering how I got your bra?"

Laura stopped in mid-stride and stared with her
mouth wide open. Was he serious? The town knew
it was a scavenger hunt. "Wouldn't they be wondering if the brassiere Reverend Pauly was waving
was his wife's?"

"Don't be ridiculous. Of course it was his wife's."

"What about the Kowalski brothers and that
nice little old lady with the walker?"

"Dammit, Laura, that's different."

"How?"

"Because, look at you!" He ran a hand through
his hair in frustration. "Look at the bra you had
on."

Laura's anger evaporated, leaving behind a harsh,
gaping wound. Josh thought she was a floozy because of her choice of undergarments. She didn't for
one moment believe the town was questioning her
relationship with him. Tears filled her eyes as she
remembered the kisses they had shared. The cop
and the floozy. It never would have worked.

"You do this town a great injustice, Josh," she said, her voice husky with unshed tears. She opened the front door and stepped out onto the sidewalk. Before closing the door she turned and added, "I hope you don't insult all newcomers like this or the town will never grow." She lowered her sunglasses and walked away, wondering what he would have thought if he'd seen the matching panties she was wearing.

Josh released the white-knuckled grip he had on the edge of the desk. It was better this way, he told himself. The gossip would die soon and the town would find something else to talk about as long as he stayed away from Laura. He watched as she disappeared into the crowd. It had taken every ounce of willpower not to take her in his arms and comfort her. He hadn't meant to hurt her, but he had. He'd seen her tears and felt a piece of his heart rip away. With a colorful curse he kicked a chair and wondered why doing the right thing hurt so much.

Laura smiled her thanks to Logan as he took the gate while she picked up assorted screwdrivers and his daughter, Ariel. They waved good-bye to Kelli and walked past a fire truck whose ladder was raised to the town clock. She kept her gaze from wandering to Josh, who was at the top of the ladder replacing the hands. "Kelli's due the end of next month, isn't she?" she asked Logan.

Logan glanced up at Josh, who was staring down and following Laura's every move. "The doctor gave her a due date of the twenty-eighth. Kelli says the baby will come on the sixteenth."

Laura chuckled. "My money's on the sixteenth." They turned down Pine Street and headed for the minister's house. "Does she still insist it's a girl?"

"Most definitely. Ariel's going to have a sister

named Elly." Logan reached over and twirled one of his daughter's blond pigtails. "So how do you like Union Station so far?"

"I love it. The people are friendly and nice." They cut through a yard and headed for the minister's white picket fence.

Logan set the gate down. "Did you enjoy the scavenger hunt?"

"It was *interesting*." Laura lowered Ariel to the ground and watched as she toddled after a butterfly. "Logan, why don't you come right out and ask me whatever it is you're dying to know?"

"What makes you think I want to know something?"

"Ever since you woke me out of bed with your phone call a year ago, demanding to know if I was the same Laura Kelli SanteFe had as a best friend at the ripe old age of eight, you have never beaten around the bush by asking dumb questions."

Logan screwed one hinge back into the post. Before attacking the other hinge, he looked up and studied Laura's face. "What happened between you and Josh?"

She quickly turned away. "That isn't any of your business."

He started to screw on the second hinge. "You're right, it isn't." He glanced over at his daughter and smiled. "It seems funny. You two were all smiles during the judging, but as soon as they announced the winner, you couldn't get away from each other fast enough." He gave the last screw a final twist. "It also seems strange that Josh nearly fell off that ladder watching you walk down the street a minute ago."

Laura repressed the feeling of happiness shooting through her. Logan had to be mistaken. "He was probably waiting for me to solicit Sylas or Harley."

Logan sat back on his heels and blinked at his wife's friend. "Pardon?"

Laura kicked a rock and grimaced. "Your friend, Josh, thinks I'm a bimbo."

"What gave him that idea?"

"My underwear."

"Were you in it or out of it?" A look of horror passed over his face and he said quickly, "No, don't answer that. Maybe you should talk to Kelli about this. On second thought, don't talk to her either. Being eight and a half months pregnant causes a few frustrations for a woman, and you might hit upon one. Hell, having a very pregnant wife causes a lot of frustrations for a man too." Seeing Laura raise her eyebrows, he added, "Don't get me wrong. I'll love Kelli till my dying breath. It's only that pregnancy places limitations on what we can do. By bedtime Kelli's too tired, during the day Ariel is up, and Kelli's the only woman I ever heard of who gets morning sickness the last three months of pregnancy."

Laura chuckled as she sat down and opened her arms for Ariel. She cuddled the girl and glanced up at the blue sky. "Isn't it a perfect day for a ride in the country? You could take your favorite girl, spread a blanket beneath a tree, and feel your frustrations fade away."

Logan grinned at some private fantasy.

"Ariel love," Laura went on, "how would you like to spend the rest of this afternoon at my house?" A chubby little fist grabbed for the sunglasses perched on her nose. "We could try to find the ghost of old man Peterson."

Logan helped Laura to her feet. "You won't mind?"

"It would be a pleasure."

Logan studied the ground and mumbled, "You could talk to Kelli before we leave."

Laura laughed. "Logan, the whole town saw my brassiere."

"The one that won the scavenger hunt?"

"That's the one I've been talking about." She chuckled as they cut back through the yard. "I won't ask what you were thinking, because I already know what your mind is focused on."

A guilty flush swept up Logan's tanned face. "How did Josh get a bimbo out of that?"

"Beats me. One minute he's the nicest guy I've ever met, and the next he's insulting the town and me."

Logan came to a halt in the middle of the sidewalk. "Are we talking about the same Josh Langley?"

Laura stopped and faced him. "Afraid so. This past weekend he threatened to throttle me, insinuated I'm a harlot, and forced me to sleep with my clothes on."

Logan leaned against the mailbox at the corner of Main and Pine and roared with laughter.

Laura stomped her foot in frustration. "You won't think it's so funny if I leave Ariel with you." She shook her finger at him. "I'm taking her home with me now only because Kelli's my friend and for some strange reason she loves you."

Logan tried to stop his laughter as visions of a lovely afternoon vanished. A silly grin and moist eyes spoiled his apology. "I'm sorry, Laura."

She picked up Ariel and started to cross the street to the park. Halfway across she turned and yelled, "And next year I'm picking my own partner for the scavenger hunt!"

"Well, I'll be damned," Logan muttered to himself. Irreproachable Josh had finally lost his composure.

Josh turned on the garden hose and walked to the birdbath he'd just finished setting back up. He held the hose still and watched as the cool water filled the bowl. The scavenger hunt was over, the park was deserted, and every piece of litter had been picked up. There was nothing else for him to do except go home to an empty apartment and watch a baseball game.

He glared at the garage apartment and wondered why it didn't look comfortable any longer. For years he had enjoyed coming home from work, kicking off his shoes, and relaxing with a beer and the latest ball game. So why was he thinking about going down to Bronco Bill's for the beer, ball game, and some company?

"Josh?"

He turned his head. "Hi, Grams. Didn't hear you come out."

"What are you doing?"

He studied his grandmother and wondered if her eyesight was going. "Giving the birds some fresh water."

"They're supposed to bathe in it, not go into diving competition."

Josh glanced down and scowled. Water was flowing over the sides of the filled bowl, creating a giant puddle. He quickly aimed the hose at a flower bed. "Sorry about that."

Ida Langley frowned at her grandson. "Congratulations again on winning the scavenger hunt." He grunted. "You must be very proud of Laura. For being a newcomer, she held up good."

Josh placed his thumb over the end of the hose and used the powerful spray to knock Japanese beetles from his grandmother's rosebushes. "Oh, yes, she was brilliant. If it wasn't for her, we wouldn't have won."

Ida cringed at the damage he was inflicting on her roses. The entire Japanese beetle population wouldn't have ruined them as much as Josh's watering. "Gladys and Bernice were saying—"

Josh whipped around to look at his grandmother. "Yes, Grams, what was Gladys and Bernice saying?"

A sad sigh escaped Ida. So that's what the problem was, she thought. Josh was waiting for the gossip to start. "They were saying they couldn't wait for Laura to start writing some articles for *The Union Station Review*. It would be a pleasant change to have some younger blood in it."

Good going, Slick, Josh told himself. Why don't you yell at your grandmother some more? "I'm sorry, Grams. I didn't mean to snap at you."

"When you were sixteen I stood by and watched as you allowed this town to run you into the ground. Half the time I think you encouraged them with your leather jacket and that black monster you called a motorcycle. You looked like the hellion everyone thought you were, but inside you were only a scared boy wondering why nobody took the time to see past the leather and long hair. Then when that Burke girl said you were the father of her child, it nearly broke your mother's and my hearts."

"Why? Neither one of you believed her."

"That's true. You denied it only once. Granted it was very loudly, but when no one listened, you gave up. You, Joshua Langley, were born with too much pride."

"Why should they have believed her over me?" His voice revealed the anger he still felt.

"Because she had the respect and wealth of her father backing her. You stood alone. Whenever your parents tried to help, you pushed them aside and faced the wagging tongues alone. You were too young and proud to accept our help."

Josh watched the spray of water hit a perfectly formed yellow rose and moved the hose lower. "So how does one earn the respect of this town?"

Ida saw the vulnerability in her grandson's face and reached for his arm. "You earned that the day you rode out of town without demanding an apology. They owed you one." She squeezed his hand. "They paid you that respect when they voted you in as sheriff after you'd been deputy for only a year."

"And last November I would have lost the election if it had been held a week later. As it was, there were petitions circulating to impeach me."

Ida chuckled. "You take things too seriously. The petitions were never presented to the town council. It was only a bunch of grown men venting their frustrations."

"My own father signed that petition!"

Ida sighed. "I was hoping you didn't know that. Look, Josh, it was the first time in twenty years that the Union Stations Tigers had a chance at the state football championship."

"Was it my fault that Tom Davis attended a pregame party and indulged in the latest domestic blend?"

"No, but he was the star quarterback. You maybe should have looked the other way and marked it down as youthful enthusiasm."

Astonished, Josh stared at his grandmother. "Tom was standing up in the backseat of Joey Taylor's convertible, doing sixty down the highway, mooning passing motorists."

"I know you were only doing your job and Tom was in the wrong. But the mayor took the loss personally. After all, Tom is his son." She reached up and kissed Josh's cheek. "I never did tell you how proud I was that you stood by your decision and didn't bow to their wishes."

A smile tugged at the corners of his mouth. "Thank you, Grams."

"I only wish you would stop acting like the *perfect* sheriff. I kind of miss the hellion. He reminds me of your grandfather when he was younger."

Love shone in Josh's eyes as he watched his

grandmother walk back to the house. She understood. He turned off the water and coiled the hose. As he climbed the stairs to his apartment, he wondered if Laura would understand, and if so, who she would fall in love with. The good sheriff, or the hellion?

There wasn't a doubt in his mind that both men had fallen in love with her.

Laura stood in the middle of her driveway and waved good-bye to Ariel. They had spent the afternoon taking a nap, building towers out of paperback books, and raiding the refrigerator. She sighed as Kelli's van disappeared down the street, then walked back up the drive. She was about to go in when she noticed the woman who lived next door working in her garden.

Laura's friendly smile slipped as she walked toward the hedge separating their yards. Low grumbling filled the air as the middle-aged woman vented her frustrations on the weeds that dared to sprout in her garden. Laura cringed as curses against the weather, bugs, and the new tax bill before the Senate came flying over the hedge. When the woman started a colorful string of comments against the welfare rolls, the homeless, and foreign trade, Laura cleared her throat.

The woman's head snapped up and blue eyes glared at her.

Laura forced a smile. "Hello, I'm Laura Bryant."

"So?"

"It seems we're neighbors."

The woman's eyes hardened. "So?"

Laura shifted uncomfortably. "I just thought I'd introduce myself." Getting no response from the woman, she said lamely, "It's been nice talking to you." She could feel the icy glare following her as she walked back across the yard.

• • •

Laura sat at her kitchen table typing up the rough draft of her article on the scavenger hunt. She had discussed it with Mrs. Billington during the cookout in the park, and they had agreed on the length and content. The sound of a car pulling into her driveway didn't register as her fingers flew over the keyboard of her old electric typewriter.

Josh stood looking in the screen door, grinning. The schoolmarm was back, with a vengeance. Her hair was piled on top of her head, a yellow pencil was stuck behind one ear, and her glasses were perched on the tip of her nose. Books and papers were scattered around her like loyal subjects ready to do her bidding.

He had returned to his empty apartment, only to be confronted by a pile of Laura's neatly folded clothes. After a quick shower, he'd picked up her belongings and hurried over. The excuse was too good to pass up. He hoped, after he explained what an idiot he was, he wouldn't need any more excuses to stop by.

Laura was startled by a knock. She rose rapidly and headed for the back door. Her bare feet slowed when she saw Josh standing there. Without opening the door she said, "Yes?"

This was going to be tougher than he'd imagined, Josh thought. "May I come in?"

She pushed her glasses to the top of her head and shrugged. "Be my guest."

He hesitantly walked in and placed her clothes on top of the dictionary. "You left these at my place."

"Thank you." She leaned against the sink and watched as he read the article sitting in the typewriter. Her heart rate quickened when a smile touched his lips. He liked it!

Surprised, he looked up and said, "Hey, this is really good."

She crossed her arms. "Well, you don't have to act so shocked," she snapped.

"I'm not shocked, just amazed." He nervously ran his hand through his hair as Laura's chin went up a notch. "I mean, who would have thought a girl like you—"

"That does it!" She marched over to the screen door and threw it open. "Out! I won't be insulted in my own house."

"Insulted?"

"That is the second time you have insinuated I'm a bimbo. Where do you get off saying such a thing? You don't even know me!"

Josh slowly walked toward her. He gazed into her eyes, which held anger and hurt, and when he spoke, his voice was soft. "I know everything I need to know about you." He stopped a foot away from her. "You're kind, gentle, and your eyes sparkle with life. Your voice gets husky when you're tired, and you have the annoying habit of being right most of the time." He reached out and traced her lower lip with one finger. "You're intelligent and have been blessed with the talent to make a simple scavenger hunt seem like the adventure of a lifetime. By next year we'll probably have people coming from as far away as Pittsburgh and Harrisburg to participate in it." His hand cupped her cheek and angled her face upward. "Your kisses are addictive and your body responds like molten fire to my every touch."

Laura's hungry gaze focused on his lips. No man had ever said such sweet things to her before. No man had dared, for the wrath of her guardian spirit had been legendary in her old hometown. Some women had reputations for being easy or cold as ice. Laura had one for being a jinx or a witch, depending on which one of her few dates was telling the story.

Josh lowered his head and lightly brushed her lips with his. "Your eyes are speaking to me, but I need to hear the words. What do you want, Laura?"

She had always considered her name to be ordinary, but when it came off Josh's lips, it sounded special, as though he were the first man ever to pronounce it correctly. "I want you to kiss me," she said, her voice trembling with desire.

A smile played at the corner of his mouth. "I thought you'd never ask," he said, and captured her sigh with a kiss.

The loud slam of the screen door filled the kitchen as Laura released it to encircle Josh's neck. Her weight shifted to the balls of her feet as she leaned up into his strength. Her mouth was moist and hungry under his tender exploration. Their tongues touched and teased. Laura heard a soft purr and was surprised when she realized it came from her.

A harsh groan from Josh answered her as he deepened the kiss and pulled her closer. Her soft breasts were crushed against the solid wall of his chest. She could feel the evidence of his arousal pressing against her stomach as his hand stroked her back. Hungry heat flowed between her thighs.

This was the feeling she had been waiting for all her life. Where had this *need* been when she had managed to be kissed by other men? Sometimes there had been pleasantness followed by curiosity, but mostly there had been disappointment. Never this burning sensation, this greedy desire.

When Josh broke the kiss with a series of small nips, she groaned in frustration. Her eyes held passion and confusion as she slowly lowered her arms and took a step back.

Josh swallowed twice and cleared his throat.

"That was nice." Hell, what was he saying? he asked himself. No way on God's good earth could that kiss be considered nice. It was explosive, hot, demanding, and Laura had matched him every step of the way. His hands clenched in frustration as his body pulsated with need.

"Would you like to go for some ice cream?" he asked roughly.

Laura blinked. "Ice cream?" Was he crazy? The man kissed her into delirium, causing untold damage to all the little hormones dashing around her body looking for something to sink their teeth into, and he offered her ice cream?

"Look, Laura, I'll spell it out for you. If we stay here for two more minutes, there will be no ice cream. There will be only you, me, and your four-poster bed."

She felt the rush of hormones gathering for the feast. "Oh."

"For years I have been acting like a gentleman. Don't let me blow it now. There is nowhere I'd rather be than in your bed, but that won't resolve our communication problem. How you figured I thought you were a bimbo is beyond me. We've known each other for only four days, so let's slow down and concentrate on being friends."

Laura marveled at his self-control as she eyed his clenched fists, straining jeans, and rapid breathing. The man was either a gentleman with morals or a masochist. Her hormones started to grumble as they headed home, and she sighed with resignation. "Double scoop?"

"Only if you ask nicely." He saw her wicked smile and headed out the door. "Put some shoes on and lock up. I'll be waiting outside."

Josh slumped against his car and breathed in the cool air. He'd had to leave the house or kiss her again. It was a heck of a decision, but he knew what would happen if he kissed her once more. He had come over that night as the noble sheriff willing to court his lady. The only problem with that was every time he kissed her, the hellion took over.

He jammed his hands into his pockets and wondered if he was schizophrenic. Sort of a Dr. Jekyll and Mr. Hyde personality. Half of him wanted to love, protect, and cherish Laura. The other half craved to know the taste of every inch of her.

Feeling restless, he walked away from the car and stared at the sky. The sun was sinking and dusk was starting to fall. It would be a perfect night for sleeping. Hell, whom was he kidding? The perfect night for sleeping was when he held a completely satisfied Laura in his arms. He muttered a curse and willed his body not to respond as she locked the door and walked toward him.

He opened the passenger door of his Corvette and Laura silently slipped in. They were driving down Main Street, heading out of town, when she disarmed him with a question. "You don't think I'm a floozy?"

"Where did you get that idea?"

"To quote, you were amazed *a girl like me* could write."

He turned the car onto the highway, driving into the sunset. "Sorry about that male chauvinist comment. It's been bred into our genes that a beautiful woman could not possibly possess a brain. It's like the old saying, date beautiful women, but never marry one. Or if your best friend is fixing you up on a blind date and tells you what a wonderful personality the woman has, you automatically think her face is one only a mother could love."

Laura laughed. "Is there a compliment buried in that?"

"Most definitely." He glanced at her. "I think

you're beautiful." He chuckled softly as a blush stained her cheeks. "Do you want to hear any more insights to the male mind?"

"Females have been handed down some valuable wisdom too."

"Name one."

"You can tell the size of a man's, umm . . . you know, from the size of his hands." She stared at Josh's hands on the wheel and felt her face grow even hotter. His hands were huge.

Josh gripped the steering wheel tighter and wished his hands would shrink. He had heard that comparison before, and it had never bothered him until a woman in some bar in Philadelphia had gawked at his hands, sat down across from him, and asked what size shoe he wore. He had quickly stood on his size twelve feet and left.

Laura noticed his tension and asked, "What about that day in your office? You said something about the town wondering how you got my bra."

Josh breathed a sigh of relief at the change of topic. "Union Station is a small town with very little excitement. When the folks get hold of some juicy gossip, they tend to blow it out of proportion. You're a beautiful single woman and I'm a single man with whom you just spent a straight thirty-six hours. Our sleeping arrangements were probably discussed over backyard fences and at the senior citizens bowling tournament. Up until that point it was all speculation and there wasn't much we could do about it. The rules clearly stated we couldn't separate. Then all of a sudden there I stood in the middle of the town square waving your bra."

Josh took a deep breath and realized he was exceeding the speed limit. "Why couldn't it have been a plain old white cotton brassiere with a tiny pink bow stitched on it? No, it had to be lace and satin. Lord, Laura, do you know there are men in this town who didn't realize brassieres can fasten in the front, let alone come in different colors?

Laura glanced out the side window and watched as they passed another farm. Great, she thought, understanding him at last. Some first impression she'd made on the town. "Is there talk?"

"Surprisingly, no. I haven't heard one word."

Her head jerked around and she glared at him. "Then what is the problem?"

"I did not like every man in town staring at your underwear!"

Seven

With a critical eye Laura stared at her reflection in the bathroom mirror. What was wrong with her? Why would a thirty-year-old man invite her miniature golfing? Couldn't he think of some safer place to take her, like a church social? The night before he'd made it quite clear he wasn't interested in picking things up from when Cal had interrupted them in the truck. Josh had checked out the house, placed a brotherly kiss on her pouting lips, and promised he would pick her up at six.

She chewed her lower lip as she finished applying another coat of mascara. Her hair was freshly washed and her cheeks held a glow of anticipation. She wore a lime green T-shirt, a pair of white shorts, green socks, and white sneakers. It was the perfect outfit for miniature golfing. It also made her look like a teenager. Was that why Josh had adopted the hands-off policy? Because she reminded him of a high school sweetheart? Well, darn it, high school sweethearts were having more fun nowadays than she was.

After one last glance in the mirror, she shrugged and headed downstairs. Josh was due any minute.

•   •   •

Josh glanced at the bouquet of flowers lying on the passenger seat and frowned. The entire town of Union Station knew by now that Josh Langley was dating Laura Bryant. And they didn't care. No gossip, no whispers, nothing. The most exciting bit of news in town was that Agnes Heckler had stood in Sanderson's Pharmacy for over an hour, going through every book on the shelves. She'd ended up buying over thirty dollars worth of paperbacks and wishing Gene a pleasant day. It was as if Josh and Laura didn't even exist. Maybe, he thought, just maybe he could start to live without watching every move he made and worrying about whom he might take down with him.

He pulled into Laura's driveway and groaned. He didn't want to go miniature golfing. He slowly walked toward the house while glancing over his shoulder at Agnes's place. Was everything all right over there? He'd be the first to admit it wasn't any of his or the town's business how many books she bought, but she had called him that morning when someone had left a basket of freshly picked blueberries on her porch. He'd jokingly told her to bake a blueberry pie with them. Maybe her admirer would stop by. Agnes had bluntly told him where to put the generous salary the town was paying him. Casting the small brick ranch house one last look, he decided to stay out of it until she asked for his help.

Laura smiled as she opened the door and let Josh in. Without saying a word, he thrust a bouquet of flowers into her hands, then hauled her into his arms. His mouth was hard and demanding as he captured her lips.

Once the initial shock wore off, Laura dissolved into his embrace. Her mouth opened, and she willingly surrendered to his demands. This was the Josh she'd been dreaming about, not the considerate gentleman who'd taken her out for ice cream the night before. Her hand tightened on the flowers as she pulled him closer.

The scratching of green tissue paper across his neck brought Josh back to the edge of sanity. He gently broke the melding of their lips and tenderly kissed her nose. "I missed you today."

Laura lowered her arms and smiled. "I'd stay away more often if that's the penalty."

He playfully swatted her rear. "Go put your flowers in water."

With loving care Laura unwrapped the bouquet and placed the flowers one by one in an old peanut jar. "Thank you, Josh. They're beautiful."

He cupped her cheek. "So are you." Her eyes darkened as he traced her high cheekbone. "Is your heart set on miniature golf?"

No, my heart's set on you. "No. I could cook us something here." She silently pleaded with him to stay. "I think I know where a deck of cards is. We could play poker or rummy."

Desire throbbed low in his abdomen. He'd fallen in love with her quick wit, the melody of her laugh, and the satiny sheen of her lower lip. He knew the honorable sheriff was going to accept the invitation, but there was always the risk the hellion would show up for dessert. "What can I do to help?"

Laura glanced at the card Josh had just laid down and grinned. She quickly snatched up the discarded queen of spades. With a flourish she placed three tens and three queens onto the rug in front of her, discarded a two of clubs, and went out. "Caught you!"

"You were holding the ten of diamonds!"

She chuckled as he turned over his cards. The

ten would have given him the hand, plus the game. She tallied up the score. He had four seventy-five to her four fifty. "One more hand should do it."

Josh grumbled as he shuffled the cards. At the distant sound of thunder, he glanced out the living room window. "It's a good thing we didn't go golfing. We never would have finished the game."

Laura got up and walked over to the window. A cool breeze was swaying the branches of the giant oak trees in her front yard. "We're going to get rain in a minute." She turned and watched as Josh dealt the cards. Dressed casually in a blue cotton shirt, faded blue jeans, and sneakers, he looked relaxed, stretched out on the handwoven rug of tranquil earth colors she had brought with her from New Mexico.

One day, when time and money came together, she'd buy furniture for the room. But for now it stood empty except for the rug, a dozen potted cacti, and Josh. A sudden flare of lightning brightened the sky, and she turned toward the stairs.

"I'll be right back. I left some windows open upstairs. Why don't you get us another soda, and there's a bag of chips in one of the kitchen cabinets."

Josh pushed himself off the floor and headed for the kitchen. He had just returned to the living room when a violent crash of lightning struck something and knocked the lights out. He heard Laura yell from upstairs that the whole town was dark. Taking care not to spill anything, he set the tray down and waited for Laura.

Rain beat against the house, lightning sparked, and thunder rolled as she slowly made her way down the dark stairs. I'll be there in a minute, Josh. I have some candles in the kitchen."

He followed her shadowy figure into the kitchen

and closed the inner door, shutting out the rain. "Summer storms are the worst," he said.

She lit two candles and passed one to him. "Do you have to go in?"

"No, Cal's on call tonight. If there's an emergency, he'll know where to reach me." He watched the play of candlelight against the walls as she walked into the living room, then chuckled as she calmly stretched out on the rug.

Enthralled Laura watched the controlled motions of Josh's hands as he finished dealing the cards by candlelight. Would they be that controlled touching her? she wondered. Would they tremble with anticipation, or burn with desire? She felt her nipples harden and a moist heat flare between her thighs. Her gaze traveled over his watch and up the length of his arm. Fine black hair feathered his forearm, the same hair that was sprinkled across his chest. She stared at the buttons on his shirt and remembered what his chest looked like the day he'd made her breakfast. Crevices and hollows had competed against rigid muscles and smooth skin for her attention.

The design on his silver belt buckle captured the light, a lone coyote howling at the moon. She was thoughtful as her gaze skimmed his powerful thighs and the length of his legs until they disappeared into the darkness beyond the candles' glow. He was beautiful, strong, and manly. Amazingly, though, it was the buckle that continued to draw her interest.

Josh noticed her fascination with his buckle—at least, he prayed it was his buckle—and asked, "Do you like it?"

"It reminds me of the Southwest," she said. "The Navaho hold great respect for the coyote."

He glanced down at the buckle and was happy he had bought it. When he'd been in Somerset that afternoon on business, he had seen it in the window of a second-hand shop. Without knowing why, he had purchased the silver buckle, replacing the perfectly good one he had with it. "The clerk assured me it was of the highest quality."

"How long have you had it?" she asked.

"About six hours." He chuckled at her expression.

"You bought it today?"

"I was leaving the courthouse in Somerset and the next thing I knew I looked up and there it was, gleaming in a window of a second-hand store. I knew I had to have it."

Laura nervously picked up her cards. The chief wouldn't have! she thought. Would he? He had never before made purchases through another person. Why should he? If Josh had bought the buckle, Josh would keep it. The chief wouldn't gain anything by it.

Her whirling thoughts calmed down. It had to be a coincidence. She drew the top card off the pile and placed it in between the cards already in her hand. Without looking, she discarded, trying to ignore the tension crackling in the air.

Josh looked at the discard and glanced back up at her. She had thrown away an ace. Either she was a brilliant strategist, or she had something else on her mind besides cards. He saw her eyes shift back to his belt buckle and willed his body not to react. The design had to be barely visible to her in the flickering candlelight, yet she still stared at it. Or at something.

The jumble of cards in her hand made no sense to Laura. The house was in total darkness, with only the immediate area around them bathed in a golden light. The house shook as the storm raged furiously. She felt her body tremble as another storm swept through her. She wanted Josh. She wanted what his kisses promised. She wanted it all.

Josh looked up from his cards as she placed hers on the rug faceup. He had his mouth open to question her when he caught the look in her eye. Heat exploded within him, and the hellion stirred to life. "Laura."

The way he said her name made her smile. Was he demanding or asking permission? It didn't matter, the answer was the same either way. She reached out and took the cards from his hand. With one quick movement she brushed the remaining cards out of the way. The only thing between them was twenty-two inches of rug.

The reflection of the candles' flames shone in her dark eyes as Josh closed the distance. His mouth demanded as his hands tenderly framed her face. She sighed as his body pressed fully against hers. With bold fingers she worked at the buttons on his shirt.

Thunder roared and the wind wailed as his shirt fell open and her soft hands stroked his back.

Josh groaned, forcing air into his lungs, then trailed heated kisses across her face. His hand reached for the hem of her shirt and slowly pulled it up. Laura lifted her back off the floor and helped him remove her shirt. She smiled at his whispered word of praise. "Beautiful."

With a trembling finger Josh circled the dark outline of her nipples through the pale lace. The candlelight illuminated her skin with a golden radiance. He smiled as the nipples hardened as if eager for his touch. A flick of his fingers and her breasts were free from their confine of satin and lace.

Impatiently, Laura pushed his shirt off his shoulders, down his arms, and flung it into the darkness. She arched her back as Josh settled between her thighs. His chest lightly brushed her rigid nipples, and a small animal sound escaped her.

Josh felt her surrender in the cradling of her

thighs. He stared down into her passion-filled eyes. "If you want to stop, Laura, it has to be now."

Her arms encircled his neck. Stop? she thought dazedly. Was he out of his mind? She applied pressure and pulled his mouth closer. "Don't you dare stop," she whispered before seizing his lips. His tongue plunged deep within her mouth as he slowly rocked his hips against hers. The fever built. Her hands trembled as she reached for his belt.

He nearly lost control when her hot fingers grazed his stomach and the front of his straining jeans. Lord! It was too much, too fast. He broke the kiss and pulled back.

"Josh?"

He rolled onto his side and lovingly traced the swell of her hip as her body instinctively followed him. "We're going to have to slow down." His voice was rough and jerky. Then, intrigued by the way the candlelight played across her breasts, he bent his dark head and grazed his lips across her nipples.

She moaned one word. "Why?"

He chuckled. "Speed is not the objective."

She sat spellbound as he finished removing her bra. With the lightest of touches, he took off her sneakers and socks and caressed her calves. In the shadowy darkness, she knew he was removing his too. She sighed as he slid back up alongside her. With his face silhouetted by the candles, he would have looked dark and hard if it weren't for the seductive fullness of his lower lip. She reached out and ran her finger over that moist lip.

A purr quivered in her throat as his teeth nipped at her finger. When he took the finger into his mouth, her stomach tightened and her hips jerked. How could there be so much need? she wondered. He was only touching her finger.

Josh's grip on his control slipped with the gentle

rocking of her hips. He rolled onto his knees and lowered her back to the ground. The sound of distant thunder filled the room. His hands shook as he unsnapped her pants and slowly peeled them down her legs. A silken triangle of white lace followed.

"Lord," he murmured, "you are lovely."

"Thank you." She heard his jeans hit the rug and the faint tearing of foil. At least one of them had come prepared, she thought, thankful the faint light hid her blush.

Laura felt the warm roughness of Josh's palms as he lightly stroked her feet and calves. She was startled when out of the darkness he placed a kiss behind her knee. Heat turned sturdy thigh muscles into quivering jelly as his fingers roamed higher. She felt a light nip on the inside of her thigh, and wetness settled at the apex of her legs.

One word hammered at Josh's brain. *Now!* He ignored the constant pounding and concentrated on the woman beneath him. His fingers combed through dark curls and sank into heaven. Moist, sweet, ready-for-him heaven. Breath lodged in his throat as she arched her hips, thrusting against his hand.

Disappointment flared through Laura as he removed his hand to clutch her hip. When his lips lowered to where his hand had been, she pulled back.

Josh smiled against her smooth stomach. He would be the first, and last, to fully taste Laura. He lifted his head to her breasts and gently suckled a nipple into his mouth.

Laura felt his arousal against her thigh, and shifted her legs farther apart. He braced himself on his arms as he positioned himself above her. His mouth tenderly coaxed her lips as he started their journey. She felt his hesitation and surprise at her tightness. She quickly wrapped her legs around him and pleaded, "Don't stop."

Josh thrust once, and stilled. Tears shimmered in her eyes. "Lord, Laura, why didn't you stop me?"

She blinked once and smiled radiantly. "I didn't want you to."

His limbs were rigid from not moving. "I hurt you."

Laura felt her muscles relax as she adjusted to his fullness. She loosened her hold on him and ran a hand down his straining back. "No. You may have caused me some discomfort, but not pain." She rocked her hips and heard him suck in a breath. "This sensation could never be considered pain."

Josh groaned and tried to remain motionless. "Don't move yet."

She thrust her hips up and sighed. She could feel him deep inside her. He was hardness to her softness, male to her female, and the answer to her dream. It had taken her twenty-eight years, but she had finally fallen in love. "Love me, Josh."

He watched her face in the soft flicker of light as he moved tentatively. Awareness, desire, and love shone there, but not discomfort. "I do love you, Laura."

He increased the tempo and captured her mouth. She matched the quick thrust of his tongue and wrapped her legs tighter around him, staying with him for every plunge. Tingling heat coiled in her stomach as the pace quickened. Her nipples ached with every brush of his chest.

Her nails dug into his shoulders as the spiraling heat exploded into a pulsating sensation, the same instant the room came alive with a clash of lightning and the deafening roar of thunder.

Josh heard her cry his name as the storm jolted the house, and thrust one last time before joining her in release.

• • •

Josh tenderly cradled Laura as he rolled off her and pulled her limp body to rest on top of his. The thunderous pounding of his heart increased as she pressed her cheek against his chest and sighed. "Are you okay?" he asked.

She placed a light kiss on his collarbone and raised her head. "Weren't you supposed to ask if it was good for me too?"

He lovingly swatted her backside. "If I have to ask, it means I failed."

She braced both hands on either side of his head and quickly kissed his smiling lips. "Let me assure you, sir, you did not fail."

Josh felt the heat of his body's response and groaned. How could he possibly need her again so soon? Her body was warm and his heaving chest cushioned her pale breasts. She was a golden goddess glistening in the candles' glow. He wanted her again, and again, and again. Was this what love was all about, constant need?

Laura closed her eyes and arched her back as Josh's hands swept over her, cupping her hips. His growing arousal nuzzled her thigh. Moisture and desire gathered between her legs as she tried to shift her weight to capture his fullness.

His hands tightened and held her still.

"Josh?"

He gulped in a lungful of air. "Don't move," he pleaded. It was too soon to love her again. He was a grown adult who should be able to control his libido. "Do you think there's any hot water left in your tank?"

"Sure, why?"

He carefully rolled out from under her and got to his feet. After cautiously handing the half-burned candles to her, he bent and picked her up.

Laura held the candles as far away as possible as

Josh carried her up the stairs. She nestled closer to Josh's chest and wondered why it felt so natural to be cradled in his arms utterly, and deliciously, naked. Where was the shyness, the hesitancy? "Can I ask where we're going?"

He climbed the last step and headed toward the bathroom. The glow of the candles cast eerie shadows down the hall. "I'm no expert, but I think a shower will help."

"Help what?"

He lowered her to the floor and glanced around the small bathroom. A pedestal sink, commode, and impressive claw-foot bathtub took up most of the room. A clear shower curtain hung from the brass rod. He placed the candles on the back of the commode and frowned at the aged pink wallpaper that sprouted fish and streams of air bubbles. In the flickering glow they reminded him of fiendish piranhas. "The soreness," he answered.

"What soreness?" she asked, fascinated that Josh was avoiding looking at her. He studied the walls, the towels, and the peeling radiator—everything but her. His blatant arousal confirmed he still wanted her, and the precious way he had handled her showed how much he cared. His current uneasiness could indicate only one thing. He was being a gentleman again. Well, hell, she didn't want the gentleman. She wanted the lover with the impatient hands and husky voice to carry her into the next room and make love to her till dawn.

With a quick twist she pinned her hair on top of her head and stepped into the tub. Not caring about the water overflow, she left the curtain parted and started the shower.

"Josh, there is no soreness." His head jerked up, and he stared at her as the warm water pounded her body. "If you really want to be a gentleman, why don't you come in here and scrub my back."

• • •

Laura snuggled deeper into the warmth of Josh's embrace. The storm had left behind cooler temperatures and gentle breezes. She opened one eye and watched as the pale light of dawn silently stretched its fingers toward the bed. Josh would be leaving soon.

When he had stepped into the tub, he had not only washed her back, but every inch of her over-heated skin. She had returned the favor with eager fingers, and if Josh noticed he smelled of lavender, he never mentioned it. They had barely dried off before he had led the way, with a lone, shimmering candle, to her bed. When they had come together for the second time, it was slow and sweet with murmured words of praise and love.

A sad sigh escaped her before she could hold it back. Josh had wanted to leave last night so no one would notice his car parked in her driveway all night. She had politely and firmly, in her best journalist terms, told him she didn't give a flying fig what the town thought. This was the nineties and they were two mature adults. If they wanted to spend the night together, dance polkas through the streets, or drink mint juleps until they fell off the porch, it was their life. She was in love for the first, last, and only time. If the townspeople didn't like it, they could all go write to their congress-man. Josh had stopped arguing, pulled her close, and fallen asleep holding her. Now, as the first finger of dawn reached the bed, Laura frowned. How did one hold back the dawn?

Glancing at Josh, one idea occurred to her. She lightly ran her palm down his chest, loving the contrast of hard muscles and soft, downy hair.

Josh came awake to the sensation of Laura's hands exploring his body. At least he hoped he was awake and that this wasn't a dream. His stomach muscles clenched as her exquisite fingers skimmed over his thighs. When she turned her head and captured his dark nipple with her lips, he stopped breathing and concentrated on the fiery sparks shooting through his body. He wanted to pull her under him and sink into her warmth, but he sensed this was a time for discovery for her. It had shocked, delighted, and humbled him last night when he'd realized he was her first lover. He had prayed he would be her last, but had never suspected he'd be the first. She was beautiful, intelligent, and utterly charming. Didn't they have men in New Mexico?

His hands curled into fists as she circled his navel with her tongue. When a lone fingernail ran up his inner thigh, discovery time had ended. He would let her explore later, when he had the strength to take it, say in five to seven years.

Laura's startled gaze flew up to Josh's face as he gripped her arms and pushed her onto her back. He loomed over her as he brought both of her hands above her head. "I think you have tortured me enough for one morning." His teeth flashed a sexy smile.

"I didn't mean to wake you," she teased.

One black eyebrow rose in response to that statement. With great care he slowly lowered his head and kissed her.

Frustration slammed through her body as Josh refused to release her hands. She wanted to touch him, hold him. The soft hair on his chest rubbed against her aching nipples, slowly driving her mad with desire. The rougher hair of his legs rasped against her smooth thighs, bringing her to a peak of insanity. She forcibly pulled her mouth away from his kisses. "Please, Josh."

He released her hands and rolled onto his back, bringing her to sit on his thighs. "This might not be the smartest thing to do in your sensitive condition," he said, tracing her full lower lip with one finger. "I won't hurt you again, Laura. You set the pace this time."

She gazed down into his serious eyes and knew what he was saying. He was allowing her to take control, to go as far as she wanted to, or could go. Well, the only discomfort she was feeling at the moment was the moist emptiness inside her crying out for fulfillment.

She leaned forward and placed a kiss on his mouth. "I love you, Joshua Franklin Langley." With lithe grace she locked her knees against his hips and started their journey toward nirvana.

Eight

Josh placed a loving kiss on Laura's swollen lips and whispered, "I'll see you tonight." She looked adorable snuggled under the blankets and cradling the pillow he had used during the night. The temptation to climb back between those sheets with her was so powerful, he jammed his hands into his pockets. It wouldn't do her reputation any good if his car were seen in her driveway at six o'clock in the morning.

She wrapped her arms around his neck and brought his mouth back to hers. "Wouldn't miss it for the world." A smile curved her lips as he reluctantly stepped back, dressed in his clothes from last night. With loving eyes she glanced down the length of his body, willing her mind to memorize every detail. A sense of uneasiness crept up her spine when her gaze encountered the silver buckle.

Josh watched her smile fade. "Laura?"

With a shake of her head she chased away the gathering dark thoughts. Her eyes sparkled with devilment as she lifted the sheet and slid over, making room for him. "Change your mind?"

He shook his head and chuckled. "Lord, woman, you are enough to tempt the devil himself."

"I don't want the devil, just the sheriff."

In one fluid motion he was sitting beside her on the bed. He cupped her cheeks and pressed a hard, quick kiss to her startled mouth. "You already have the sheriff, lady." The rough pads of his thumbs caressed her cheekbones. "I love you, Laura."

She closed her eyes in ecstasy. By the time she reopened them he was gone. She heard the faint closing of the kitchen door and the quiet hum of his car as he drove away. With gleeful abandonment, she buried her face in his pillow. It smelled of lavender, loving, and Josh.

Her radiant smile dimmed as she remembered the one puzzle piece that didn't belong in her happily-ever-after. The silver belt buckle with the lone wolf. Why did Josh buy it? Was it just a whim, or was a certain someone behind it? Like Chief Snuggle Bear.

Laura was dressed for work and reaching for her second cup of coffee when a light knock on the kitchen door interrupted her musing. She hid her surprise and placed a welcoming smile on her lips as she greeted her neighbor, Agnes Heckler. "Good morning, Ms. Heckler, won't you come in?"

The older woman hesitated slightly before entering the kitchen. She held out a small basket to Laura. "I came over to apologize."

Folding back the fine blue linen napkin that covered the basket, Laura stared in confusion at half a dozen blueberry muffins. "For what?" she asked.

"The other day you came over being friendly and introduced yourself." Agnes tilted her head up proudly. "I behaved dreadfully, and I'm sorry for that. Sometimes a person has to hit rock bottom before they realize they have fallen. I baked a batch of blueberry muffins this morning as a peace offering."

Laura saw the uncertainty clouding her neighbor's eyes and smiled. "We all have bad days."

Tears clogged Agnes's throat. "Some of us have bad years."

Quick compassion and understanding bonded the two completely different but remarkably similar women. Laura had heard from Josh how Agnes had lost her husband and only child nine years earlier in a car accident, and had withdrawn from the world. Laura had lost her family and fought against the world. Laura's bad years had ended when she acquired her guardian spirit, and if she weren't off the mark, Agnes's were starting to end.

"Some of us had reasons," she said, and watched as Agnes rapidly blinked back her tears. "I would love to accept your unnecessary peace offering, on one condition."

"What is that?"

"You'll join me in a cup of coffee. I have an hour yet before I'm due at work."

Agnes sat down uncertainly at the table, as if she were unsure of what to expect. "I have a few moments of free time."

Laura quickly poured a fresh cup of coffee and set it down in front of Agnes. "Your gardens are wonderful. Hopefully by next spring I'll be ready to start one of my own."

Agnes looked astonished, as if the idea of planting gorgeous blooming flowers around the exterior of a haunted house was unheard of. She accepted one of her own muffins and asked, "Are you fond of gardening?"

The next ten minutes were taken up by discussions of various flowers and herbs. Agnes finished her cup of coffee and studied the bouquet of flowers gracing the table. "They're beautiful. I bet you got them at Claudia's."

"I'm not sure where they came from. They were given to me."

A knowing smile lit up Agnes's face. "Josh Langley?"

Laura fought the blush stealing up her cheeks. "Yes."

"He's a fine boy, Laura. Don't listen to those stories about him."

"What stories?" she asked, intrigued.

Agnes was momentarily thrown off balance. "I'm sorry, that was years ago. I guess with him being the sheriff and all, the rumors have stopped."

"Which rumors were they?" Laura asked, even as she battled her conscience. She should be asking Josh about the old stories, not begging a neighbor. But this was love, and wasn't everything fair in war and love?

"They called him the hellion," Agnes said. "I could never figure what he ever had done that was wrong, but he did dress the part. Black leather jacket, tight jeans, and boots. His hair was long, and by the time he was sixteen he was shaving. The only thing that didn't hold true to his image was his eyes. They were crystal-clear blue and kind. He never smiled, except with those eyes. I don't think anyone paid attention to them. One day I came out of the bank and he was leaning against a lamppost with this fierce expression on his face, watching a group of girls walk by. But there was a look of sadness and loneliness in his eyes. A few weeks later I saw him wearing dark sunglasses.

"He used to ride this dangerous black motorcycle that gleamed of chrome and had red flames painted on the side of the gas tank. Under those flames he had the word *Hellion* painted. He was every girl's fantasy, and every mother's nightmare.

One afternoon I had a flat tire out on the highway into town. For over an hour I had struggled to loosen lug nuts while cars whizzed by. Josh was the only one who stopped to give me a hand. He changed the tire and refused any sort of payment. Even with all those nasty stories spreading about how he got Julie Burke in trouble, I knew he was a good boy."

Laura took a moment to mull over what Agnes had told her, then exclaimed, "Josh has a child!"

"Lord, no. It turned out Julie had just pointed her high-class finger at the town's bad boy, Josh. Daddy naturally believed her and came down heavy on Josh. I think it was a couple of weeks later when the truth came out and Josh was cleared."

Laura now understood why Josh was concerned with what people thought. His teenage years had been shaped and scarred by the town's gossip. Impulsively she covered Agnes's hand. "Thank you, Agnes."

Agnes turned her palm up and squeezed Laura's hand. "You're welcome." She stood up. "I better get going so that you can get ready. Where do you work?"

"I'm working for Mrs. Billington at *The Union Station Review*. I'm the new reporter."

"About time this town got some new blood. Now I can look forward to reading the paper on Wednesdays."

"Thanks for the muffins, they were delicious."

"Anytime." Agnes walked over to the screen door and stopped. "Can I ask a personal question?"

Laura nervously shifted her feet. "Sure."

"You said you came from New Mexico." Seeing Laura nod, she asked, "Are there a lot of Indians in New Mexico?"

Sweat broke out across Laura's brow. "Yes."

"Do you think they're as good lovers as those romance books make them out to be?"

Laura's mouth fell open, and not a sound came out.

"I'm sorry, Laura. I didn't mean to embarrass you."

"No, no, Agnes, you didn't embarrass me. Stun, definitely, shock maybe, but not embarrass." Laura desperately clutched the basket of remaining muffins. "I'm sorry, but I can't answer that question by experience. Still, I don't think it matters what nationality you are. If two people love each other, then it's the right combination."

Agnes's stare was long and hard before a soft smile curved her mouth. "I do believe you're right, Laura. Thank you."

Laura stood at the screen door and watched as Agnes made her way between the hedges into her own yard. What in the world was that all about? She stared down at the four blueberry muffins nestled in the basket and frowned.

Curious, she climbed the two flights of stairs to the chief's room. His door was open and sunlight streamed in through the windows. The large steamer trunk was wide open and empty.

Laura sat down in the middle of the floor and reached for the only non-Indian item in the room—a tattered teddy bear. She clutched the bear to her breasts, drawing strength from it. She had received the crazy teddy bear for her fifth birthday from her parents and had lovingly christened him Snuggle Bear. It was the last thing her parents had ever bought her. A few weeks later they were killed in a car accident, leaving behind a bewildered five-year-old daughter, a handful of photographs, and not enough memories.

Snuggle Bear was her constant companion in the years that followed her parents' death. Somehow it made her feel close to them. When she acquired her guardian spirit, she asked him to give her a clue to his name. Every night Snuggle Bear was moved from his place of honor, on top of her bureau, to the kitchen table. Mischievously, she named her guardian spirit Chief Snuggle Bear.

Laura glanced around the room and marveled at the belongings the chief had gathered in the past ten years. Baskets, a woven wool blanket of vivid red, assorted arrows, and two bows. All of the chief's possessions had cost her a pretty penny. Not only did he have an eye for quality, he had no concept of what payday meant. Laura had found herself more than once signing a credit card slip while arguing with thin air.

Her jewelry box contained so much silver and turquoise jewelry, she could have a silver mine named in her honor. After years of pleading with the chief, she had finally convinced him to buy within her budget. He'd broken the rule only once, and that was the week before they left New Mexico. A silver and turquoise hand mirror, brush, and comb now graced the top of her bureau instead of Snuggle Bear.

Thinking of that purchase reminded her of Josh's new belt buckle. "Chief Snuggle Bear, leave Josh alone! I'm not sure what you might be up to, but you'd better not be interfering with what's happening between us." Exasperated, she stood and gently placed the teddy bear on the windowsill. "I want you to listen and listen well. Leave Agnes Heckler alone. I don't know why she asked about Indians, and I'd rather not. Let's just say it better not have anything to do with you."

She walked to the door and stomped her foot. "I might not know how to send you back, but by hell I know how to summon up another guardian spirit if the need arises! So, don't push your luck. He just might be bigger than you."

• • •

Josh reached over the gear shift and threaded his fingers with Laura's. "When I said to dress casual, I meant *casual*, not heart-stopping sexy. How am I supposed to enjoy myself if I have to break a barstool over the head of every man who looks at you?"

Laura chuckled. "I think there's a compliment in there somewhere. Thank you." She glanced down at her faded jeans, yellow camisole top, and over-size man's cotton shirt, which she'd left unbuttoned with its shirt-tails tied around her waist. Lord, the man had to be blind. Sexy was what *he* did to a pair of jeans.

When she had opened her door earlier, it had taken every ounce of willpower she possessed not to drag him up to her bedroom. Seeing the gleam in his eye, she'd guessed he felt the same. They had settled for one hot, demanding kiss before quickly leaving the house. Tonight Josh was taking her to Bronco Bill's for dinner and dancing. He wanted to introduce her to Union Station's hottest nightspot.

He parked the Corvette in the farthest slot away from the battered pickup trucks. "There's not a whole lot to choose from on the menu, but the food is great."

Laura got out of the car and grinned. "Let me guess. There's steak."

"Umm-hmm."

"And steak."

"Umm-hmm."

"And, my favorite, steak."

Josh laughed and grabbed her hand. "You do get a choice between burnt and raw."

She stopped in front of him and wrapped her arms around his waist. "Does this piece of carnivorous bliss come with a baked potato smothered in sour cream or huge, monstrous home fries?"

"Right the second time."

"Served with a salad and ranch-style dressing."

"I think you must have eaten here before."

"Nope. We had a place like this outside Santa Fe. It was called The Hole."

He bent and placed a quick kiss on the corner of her mouth. "I bet it didn't have Milly's famous buttermilk biscuits."

"Real buttermilk biscuits?" she whispered in awe.

"The best."

"What are we waiting for?"

Josh laughed as she pulled him across the parking lot and toward the entrance.

Laura pushed her plate away and groaned. "I may never stand again."

Josh grinned as he finished the last of his coffee and glanced at the dance floor. "We can dance it off."

Her heart gave a sudden leap as she studied the dancers entwined in one another's arms, slowly swaying to the music. "I would like that."

Josh's body reacted to the huskiness of her voice. He pushed his chair back and held out his hand. Without hesitation she stood and took it.

When Josh pulled her into his arms and started to dance, a sigh eased past her lips. Heaven was being cradled in Josh's embrace while dancing on a worn oak floor. A Willie Nelson song about a woman always being on his mind echoed off the wood-planked walls, wrapping the dancers in a seductive cocoon. The sounds of the clattering plates, rattling silverware, and mingling voices disappeared into oblivion. There was just Josh, her, and the sweet, slow rhythm of a country love song.

The pounding of Josh's heart settled into a deep even beat. The physical awareness of Laura pressed against his body was leveling off to a dull throb. The contentment that inhabited him came from Laura herself, not what her body felt like under his. She was bright, possessed a wicked sense of humor, and projected the air of someone who understood the secrets of the universe and could live with them. He savored her cooking, but would have loved her even if she couldn't manage to butter toast. She had bought a house that was reportedly haunted and pedaled a bright yellow bicycle to work every day. Material possessions didn't seem to make a big impression on her. The only signs of extravagance he'd seen was her hand mirror and brush set, and her jewelry. The silver necklace hanging around her neck looked expensive.

He gently brushed her hair away from her ear and placed a string of kisses up her jaw to her lobe, where a matching set of silver earrings dangled. Tomorrow he'd ask Kelli for the name of the jeweler in Santa Fe who had made the necklace Logan had bought for her out there. Laura would appreciate the high-quality craftsmanship.

"Have I told you how beautiful you are?" he murmured.

"You did mention something about sexy as hell." With a mischievous smile, she added, "But you could elaborate."

He tugged her closer and subtly moved his hips against her. Laura released the small whimper in her throat. She could feel him ready and hard. "Lord, Sheriff, when you elaborate, you really *elaborate*."

Laura pulled the sheets up over her head. "Josh, turn off the light and come back to bed."

A masculine chuckle filled the room as he sat down on the bed to put on his sneakers. "It's almost dawn."

She covered a yawn, then mumbled, "Tell me something I don't already know." Dawn was definitely becoming a hateful four-letter word.

"I'm picking you up at six tonight and we're having dinner at my place." He determinedly lowered the sheet and kissed her lips. "I'm on duty this weekend, so I have to stay close by. You don't mind, do you?" He anxiously watched her expression.

Supple tanned arms wrapped around his neck, pulling him closer. "No, I don't mind having dinner with you tonight." Her kiss stopped his words.

Josh broke the kiss and groaned. "That's not what I meant."

"I know." She pushed back a lock of his hair. "You were asking me if I mind being stuck in town while you're on duty. Being the sheriff is who you are, it's part of you. When I fell in love with you, I fell for all of you, not just the convenient parts."

Reverence filled his soul. "Thank you." He brushed his mouth across hers. When she responded readily, he deepened the kiss.

Laura nipped at his lower lip and felt him shudder. Her hands impatiently pulled his shirt from his jeans and caressed his smooth back. The cool morning air flowed over her breasts as he tugged the sheet lower.

She cried out when his warm mouth released hers to burn a path of desire down her neck to her aching breasts.

His face buried against her breasts, he muttered, "I have to get going, Laura."

She sank her teeth into her bottom lip. The dawn had won. Again. "I know." She understood that he was trying to protect her against the wagging tongues in town, but it still hurt. Everyone knew they were seeing each other, so who would care if his car was parked in her driveway come morning? "I'll see you at six."

The fragrance of lavender stirred his senses. He slowly raised his head and studied the face of the woman he loved. She was gorgeous with her hair in wild disarray, spread out across the pillow. Her eyes were dark with desire, her lips red from his kisses. For one crazy moment he was tempted to ask her to marry him. He'd known her for two weeks and already couldn't imagine his life without her. The thought of waking every morning with her beside him caused a slow smile to spread across his lips. She deserved more than a hurried proposal and a mad dash to the altar. He wanted to give her moonlight and poetry. He wanted to buy her expensive gifts and drink champagne for breakfast. He wanted to give her the best courtship any woman had ever had. *He wanted forever.*

Laura gasped in surprise as Josh pressed against her and kissed her fiercely. Her body softened and her thighs parted to cradle his jean-clad leg.

His breathing was quick and uneven as he broke the kiss and stood. "I'll pick you up at six."

Her answering smile faded as his footsteps drifted down the stairs and out the door. With a feeling of dread she lifted the sheet off her hip and studied the faint red mark his belt buckle had left.

Tears filled her eyes as she slowly traced the fading mark. What was she going to do if the chief were somehow controlling Josh's feelings? It did seem strange that the chief even allowed Josh to kiss her, let alone actually make love to her. She had been expecting earthquakes or typhoons to wipe the entire town of Union Station off the map. But what did she get? Silence. No drums, no shaking walls, not even a demented grasshopper to terrorize her suitor.

Great. That could mean the chief was finally allowing her to live her own life and make her own mistakes. Or, he was manipulating Josh into thinking he was in love with her. Or—and this was the explanation she was praying with all her heart for—Josh really did love her and the chief had actually guarded her through all those years, keeping her safe and protected for Josh.

Laura blinked back her tears. There was only one way of knowing, and that was time. If the chief was controlling Josh, there would be some sort of sign besides a buckle. There had to be.

Nine

Laura glanced around her kitchen and frowned.
What was with Josh tonight? They had shared a
very enjoyable meal at his apartment, complete
with wine, music, and candlelight. After the
dishes were stacked in the dishwasher, they had
snuggled on his couch and watched a movie he
had rented about giant worms who terrorized an
entire town. Halfway through the movie they were
cheering the worms on.

When the movie ended, Josh had calmly turned
off the VCR and announced it was getting late.
Shortly thereafter, Laura had found herself standing in her own kitchen while Josh checked her
house for criminals committing untold violations.

"All clear," he announced, returning to the
kitchen.

She placed her pocketbook on the table. "Is it
really necessary for you to peek into my closets and
under the bed every time you bring me home?"

"I need to know you're safe before I can leave."

"Are you leaving?" That's class, old gal, she
thought. Why don't you just ask him to spend the
night doing spectacular things to your body?

His movements stiff, Josh walked to the door and grabbed the knob. "It's getting late."

Laura was bewildered. "All right." If there ever was a man eager to leave, it was Josh. "Will I see you tomorrow?" she asked uncertainly.

He quickly returned to her and placed a kiss on the tip of her nose. "How does dinner at Emma's sound?"

"I could cook us something here."

"No, you work all day." He bent and lightly kissed her mouth. "I'll see you about six."

Josh walked out of the house and into the darkness, hurrying to his car. That was a close one, he thought as he backed out of her driveway. One more minute and he would have swept her up into his arms and carried her to bed. He knew she was confused, but that couldn't be helped at the moment. He was going to woo her into becoming Mrs. Joshua Langley.

"I'm telling you, Agnes, that outfit is stunning on you. Whoever designed it had you in mind." Laura smiled as the woman standing in front of the full-length mirror blushed.

"Are you sure, Laura? I haven't bought clothes in years and the styles look so different."

Laura smiled at Agnes. When the older woman had asked if she would go shopping for clothes with her, she had jumped at the chance to occupy her mind with something besides Josh's odd behavior. "All you've bought so far are jeans and tops for work. I think it's wonderful that you took a part-time job at Claudia's greenhouse. But suppose you have to go somewhere else, what would you wear?"

Agnes shifted her gaze back to the mirror. Her body was still trim and firm. With her height of five feet seven, she wore the outfit with style. Pleated trousers and a matching jacket in deep plum were highlighted by a pink sleeveless top. It was simple and chic. With a nervous hand she brushed back her brown hair, which was sparsely tinted with gray. "Did I tell you I have an appointment Monday night to have my hair done?"

Laura laughed, hustled her back into the dressing room, and nodded to the anxious saleswoman.

If you went by the number of packages they loaded into Agnes's car, the trip seemed to be a success. If you looked at the excitement shimmering in Agnes's eyes, you knew it was.

Josh pulled out a chair and made Kelli sit down. Just looking at her enlarged belly gave him a backache. "Are you sure?" he asked.

"Of course I'm sure. I ought to know when Laura's birthday is, and it's Friday."

"Well, why didn't she tell me?"

"Josh, no one goes around telling people when their birthday is. It would be like asking for presents."

"Do you think I can get the necklace in time?"

"Pick up the phone and see if they can airmail it out today. You should get it Thursday, Friday at the latest."

With a motherly sigh Kelli watched as Josh headed toward the phone. *What would men do without us?* she wondered.

Josh sat in the barber chair and glanced up at Ed. "Just a little off the back." He settled down and mentally went through the growing list of things to be done before tomorrow night. Agnes and Mrs. Billington were handling the food. Kelli and Logan were in charge of the decorations, and Sylas was bringing the music. The cake would be delivered the next afternoon and the necklace had arrived that morning. All that was left was making sure Laura didn't find out.

A sharp jab to the back of his neck brought Josh out of his musing. "Ouch, watch it, Ed." He reached up and rubbed the tender spot, then turned in time to see what had caught Ed's attention. Agnes was strolling along the sidewalk. Josh studied Ed's dazed look and smiled. The love bug was working overtime this summer. "Ed, old man, how would you like to come to a party tomorrow night?"

"It's dreadful, Laura. Simply dreadful," Agnes cried.

Laura's grip tightened on the phone. "What's wrong?"

"Come quick, Laura. It's horrible."

Laura slammed the phone back onto its cradle. Something was wrong with Agnes! She raced through the kitchen door and across the backyard. After squeezing through the opening in the hedges, she ran to Agnes's sliding glass doors, slid them open, and froze.

"Surprise!"

Laura stared openmouthed as numerous people threw confetti and raised champagne glasses to her. Agnes grabbed her hand and dragged her into the living room, where someone placed a full glass of champagne in her hand. Streamers and balloons decorated every available surface.

Josh pulled Laura against him and placed a kiss on her still-open mouth. "Happy birthday, sweetheart."

Laura forced a smile and glanced around the room for the one person who knew it was *not* her birthday. Kelli. She spotted her grinning and reclining in an armchair with her feet propped up on a hassock. "Excuse me a moment, Josh."

With extreme care Laura helped Kelli to her feet. "You don't mind if I borrow your wife for a moment, Logan, do you?" Before Logan could answer, she hauled the waddling Kelli into the first empty room.

Kelli glanced around the tiny bathroom with amusement. Even with her back pressed against the wall, her belly took up most of the room.

Laura managed to squeeze in and closed the door. "What in the hell did you do?" she whispered fiercely. If it were possible to reach past the extended belly, she would have wrapped her hands around Kelli's throat.

"Josh wanted to do something special for you. He needed this."

"I'm not understanding a thing you're saying, Kelli. You have exactly one minute to explain why you told Josh it was my birthday."

Kelli shifted her weight and sat on the edge of the tub. "Josh is my dearest friend. When he was young, this town hurt him badly. It robbed him of his self-respect when he was the most vulnerable. He came back here to win that respect, and he did. The only problem is he hasn't realized it yet. The old insecurities still crop up once in a while."

Laura saw love for Josh in Kelli's eyes, a different love from what she felt for him, but love nevertheless. "I know that, Kelli. I still don't see how this party helps him."

"This is the first thing he's initiated since the petitions for his impeachment were circulated."

"Impeachment?"

"It was a slight mixup concerning the arrest of the mayor's son. Don't look so worried. The petitions never made it to the town council. It was only a bunch of grown men crying over a lost football game. The town soon forgot about the petitions, but Josh didn't."

"I can't imagine why!" Laura snapped.

"Calm down, Laura. Josh is so proud of this party. He had Agnes, Mrs. Billington, and me help with the preparations, but he invited everyone. You should have seen his face when he was telling me who accepted. Everyone accepted, and people were coming up to him on the streets trying to wangle an invite. I think he's beginning to believe the town does like him."

Laura bit her lip. "So what you're telling me is that if I go out there and tell them it's not my birthday, it not only embarrasses me, but it humiliates Josh."

"I think you love him enough not to do that." Reaching behind her to brace herself on the other rim of the tub, Kelli's eyes widened as she slowly sank into the tub.

Laura chuckled at the picture Kelli made with her legs and arms dangling over the tub. Her rounded belly rose above the rim like a mountain. "I have never purposely humiliated another human being in my life. I guess I'm too old to start now, considering I'm now twenty-nine."

Kelli smiled and held out her hand. "Help me out of here."

Laura's smile turned into a full-blown grin. "I think not."

"Laura, come on." Kelli struggled for leverage and failed. "What would I tell people if they saw me like this?"

"The same thing I'm going to have to say on October fifteenth, when it really is my birthday." With a chuckle she opened the door and left her friend to stew.

On her way back to the living room she spotted Logan and relented. "Your wife needs you in the bathroom down the hall," she told him. Okay, she thought, so she had a soft heart for pregnant women.

Josh looked up the moment Laura entered the room. He made his excuses to the mayor and hurried over to her. "Is everything all right?"

She smiled. "What could possibly be wrong? I'm another year older, and before long I'll be sprouting gray hairs."

He chuckled and wrapped his arm around her waist.

Half an hour later Laura was opening the last gift. Talk about life's embarrassing moments, she thought. She was still waiting for the police to come and arrest her for false representation, except the local police had his arm around her and was whispering suggestive ideas in her ear.

Laura sighed as she thanked Mrs. Billington for the set of quilted placemats. She was reaching for her glass of champagne when Josh placed a brightly wrapped package in her hand. Studying the box, she realized this was going to be worse than she thought.

Her fingers trembled as she slipped the pink bow off. Whatever the gift was, it was heavy. She peeled the shimmery paper back and studied the red box. With an encouraging look from Josh, she lifted the lid. Her heart slammed to a halt as she pulled out a large black velvet jewelry box. Every woman's fantasy present was turning into her own personal nightmare. The room went deadly silent as she slowly lifted the lid. Inside, nestled on a bed of black velvet, was a flawless Indian squash-blossom necklace. Sterling silver shimmered and the turquoise nuggets gleamed with a life of their own. It was exquisite, perfect, and, she knew, extremely expensive. *Just the kind of present the chief would have picked.*

Josh shifted nervously as Laura sat motionless. He was hoping for a more emotional response, like her throwing her arms around his neck and declaring her undying love for eternity. "Laura?"

She blinked back tears that threatened to overflow. This was the sign she'd been praying would never come. Her voice was husky with tears as she whispered, "I can't accept this."

"Why not?" he asked, startled.

Everyone was staring at her. Shrugging, she said, "It's too expensive."

Josh released the breath he'd been holding and laughed. "Is that all?" With cheers from the crowd, he led Laura, who still held the box, onto the back patio. The applause was muffled as he slid the patio doors closed.

Laura glanced nervously at the colored plastic lights strung around the slate patio and wished she were anywhere but there. Nicaragua had some appealing tourist packages this time of year. Then again, the Falkland Islands were offering extended "Tan your can" weekend excursions.

Warm palms framed her face as Josh gazed at her in the fading light. "Do you like the necklace?"

"It's a beautiful piece of art and any woman would be proud to wear it," she said honestly.

"I'm hearing a 'but' in there."

How could she explain that not only wasn't it her birthday, but he really hadn't bought the necklace for her? Defeated, she said, "It's just *too* expensive."

"No, it wasn't. It cost only money." He placed a kiss on her trembling lips. "I wanted something special for you because you are special to me. I love you, Laura." His thumbs wiped at the tears rolling down her cheeks. "I've never said that to another woman."

Laura stood on her toes and melted into his arms. *Who would it hurt to believe for just a little while longer?*

• • •

Josh placed the last of Laura's presents on her table and smiled. The party had been a huge success. Why hadn't he ever noticed before how the mayor often ran ideas by him? Maybe he was finally forgiven for locking up Tom. "That's the last of your haul, birthday girl."

Laura mustered a weak smile. "Thank you, Josh, for everything."

He frowned as she rubbed her temple. "Headache?"

Headache, hell, she thought. It felt like an ice pick was sticking into her forehead. "I must have drunk too much champagne."

Josh pulled the leash on his raging hormones. Tonight was not the night. He couldn't complain since he was the one who had put a halt to their lovemaking several days before. He knew Laura was confused by his actions, but when he would ask her to become his wife, he wanted her answer based on something more than what they could share in bed. "Why don't you take a couple of aspirin and go to sleep? You've had a busy day."

"I will." She walked him to the door. "Was I imagining it, or were Agnes and our Cossack barber making eyes at each other all night?"

"Eyes? Hell, woman, the heat those two were generating was melting the Chinese lanterns strung around her yard." He pulled her into his arms and kissed her. "I'll call you tomorrow. Take care of that head."

Laura's composure dropped as the door closed behind Josh. Tears rolled down her cheeks as she lovingly caressed the necklace fastened around her neck.

Josh gazed out his office window at the park across the street. The local Boy Scouts had set up a carnival to raise money for a little boy over in Somerset who needed an operation. They were doing a brisk business selling hot dogs, soda, and funnel cakes. For a small fee you could have your face painted by the scout master, or try your luck at the bean-bag toss, ring toss, or darts. A bald tire hung from a tree, and if you could chuck a football through the opening, you would win your sweetheart a plastic beaded bracelet. Agnes had volunteered to be Madame Swami, and she'd read your palm for a quarter.

He chuckled as Ed entered Madame Swami's tent again. That was the fifth time he'd had his palm read. Josh straightened as he spotted a familiar figure making its way from game to game. Laura! He'd known she wouldn't be able to resist the temptation of a carnival.

"I'm heading across the street, Cal," he said to the deputy. "Why don't you finish here, lock up, and head on home." He ignored Cal's knowing smile as he closed the door and crossed Main Street.

The camera jerked in Laura's hands as Josh came up behind her. He hadn't made a sound or touched her, but she knew he was there. She concentrated on looking through the camera at the freckled faced boy scout running the ring toss game. She clicked a series of pictures and hoped one would turn out. Photography wasn't one of her strong points, so she figured that quantity was important. If she shot a few rolls of film, one or two pictures had to be good enough to print.

She smiled and turned to look at Josh. "Hi." Every nerve ending in her entire body was screaming for his touch, but she willed herself not to respond to his nearness. For the past week he had been blowing hot and cold. His hungry good-night kisses tortured her with promises, yet he always left before they could build into her secret fantasy.

Why hadn't they made love since the night at Bronco Bill's?

"Hi, yourself," he said. On impulse he brushed a lock of her hair behind her ear. "I see you're working. Am I allowed to buy the next Ansel Adams lunch?"

"I have a few more pictures to take, but then I'm free." She walked up to the next booth and studied the different angles. Wallets, keychains, and leather belts were spread out across a table. Group pictures, posters, and the latest troop information were stapled to the three walls of the booth. An eager young boy was smiling hopefully at her from behind the table.

Josh moved out of Laura's way and picked up a fascinating leather and beadwork belt. He ran his fingers over the brightly colored beads and marveled at the design. A one-eyed thunderbird spread his wings, multicolored arrows pointed in different directions, and bolts of lightning zagged. Who cared that there were gaps between the beads and that the thunderbird's head was off center? It was a beautiful piece of craftsmanship, nonetheless.

Excited, he held the belt out and eyed the length. It was perfect for Laura. The Indian motif would blend with her usual style of clothes. He reached into his wallet and placed several bills in the young boy's hands.

Laura grinned as she snapped candid shots of the boy. In the back of her mind it registered that Josh had just purchased something from the table, but she was so engrossed in capturing the boy's expressions on film, she failed to notice what. She lowered the camera and studied the leather keychains. The designs were crude and childish, but they were made with heart. She selected the largest one to attach to her keys that always got lost in the bottom of her handbag. The boy stuttered, "Thank you," when she handed him four dollars.

Josh led her around the side of the booth and away from the main flow of traffic. "I found something that was crying out your name," he said, then handed her the belt and waited.

Laura glanced down at the amateurish belt. "You bought this for me?"

His voice was enthusiastic as he started to point out the finer points. "Look at the border, see how they alternated the colors? And check out the thunderbird, isn't he magnificent?"

Her fingers trembled as she held the belt. She examined the beadwork with tear-filled eyes. Josh thought this belt was the pinnacle of Indian workmanship! She tenderly traced the crooked arrows and the mismatched colored designs. The chief would turn his broad nose up in the air over such childish quality!

Josh hooked his finger under her chin and raised her tear-streaked face. "Laura, don't you like the belt?"

"I think it's the most wonderful present I've ever received in my life."

He stumbled back as she flew into his arms and kissed him. Regaining his balance, he welcomed her warmth.

Laura broke the kiss and tenderly caressed his cheek. She read desire, need, and love burning in the depth of his eyes. With absolute certainty she knew the chief was not behind Josh's feelings. Josh loved her for herself, and the chief had politely kept his theatrics to himself. Her voice was thick with tears of happiness as she whispered, "I love you."

Heat raged within Josh as he pulled her into his arms and sealed her mouth with his. This was what he'd missed in the past week. The hell with being a gentleman. He wanted Laura. And he wanted her now. She could make up her mind between cotton sheets if she wanted to become Mrs. Joshua Langley. Then again, he could always keep her there until she gave the correct answer.

When the distant sound of voices penetrated his dazed brain, he pulled back and glanced around. Amazingly, no one seemed to notice their sheriff was an ant's toe away from making love to Laura in the middle of a fund-raiser. Putting some desperately needed inches between them, he asked, "Can you keep that thought for an hour?"

"I can keep *that* thought for the rest of my life."

He opened his mouth to say something just as Ed walked around the side of the booth. "There you be, Laura," Ed said. "Come and take picture of Madame Swami and me."

A low grumble came from Josh's chest as he positioned Laura in front of him and followed the beaming Cossack to the fortune-teller's tent.

Josh rolled over and fumbled for the ringing phone. Bringing the receiver up into the general vicinity of his ear, he mumbled, "'Lo."

"Josh, this is Bill. Sorry for disturbing you, but you better get down here fast."

Josh instantly sat up and glanced down at the waking woman beside him. "What's wrong?"

"Daryl's drunk again." Josh could hear an uproar of noise in the background. "I'm going to try to reach Cal too. I've never seen Daryl this bad before."

"Okay, Bill. I'm on my way. Just try to keep everyone out of his way till I get there." He dropped the phone in its cradle and got out of bed.

Laura watched as he hurriedly pulled on his uniform, which he had been wearing at the carnival that afternoon. "What's wrong?"

He buttoned his shirt and jammed it into his

pants. "One of the local's consumed more alcohol than his system can take. He's threatening to tear Bronco Bill's apart."

She slid over to make room for Josh on the bed as he pulled on his socks and shoes. "Is he dangerous?"

"Not physically. Daryl's wife left him a couple of months ago, so about every two weeks he shows up drunk at Bronco Bill's." Josh leaned over and kissed her. "Go back to sleep. I'll take your keys and let myself in after I settle Daryl down."

The sheet fell to her waist, exposing her breasts as she wrapped her arms around his neck. "Take care and hurry back."

He kissed her moist, willing lips and groaned. "You're not playing fair, Laura. How am I supposed to leave when you look like this?"

"I'll be looking like this when you get back. Now, go and make sure nothing happens to Bronco Bill's. I love the way you move your hips when we slow-dance there."

A silly grin spread across Josh's face as he hurried out to his car. Life didn't get any better than this.

"Come on, Daryl," Josh said in a calm voice. "Put the stick down." Josh had entered the bar and taken in the scene with a glance. Daryl was alone in the bar area looking drunk, confused, and lonely. The other customers had moved out onto the dance floor and were acting as if nothing out of the ordinary was happening. Everyone knew about Daryl's wife, Joleen, walking out and leaving behind their three children. Daryl owned a small farm, was a deacon at the local church, and had never indulged in liquor until a couple of months earlier.

Josh quietly pulled out a barstool and sat. He

kept an eye on Daryl in the mirror behind the bar and looked at Bill. "Coke, please."

Bill placed the soft drink in front of Josh and went on wiping down the bar.

"She was a good woman!" Daryl shouted.

Josh looked into his glass. He had his own thoughts on the subject of a wife and mother deserting her family to take up with an insurance salesman from Potter County.

The stick slammed down on the top of a table. Daryl's voice rose another decibel. "She was a good mother!"

Josh kept his head down but carefully watched Daryl in the mirror. If Daryl followed his usual pattern, he'd rant on about Joleen's virtues for a couple of minutes, then sit down and bawl like a baby. That was when Josh or Cal drove him home and with the help of his parents, who had moved back to the farm when Joleen left, put him to bed.

Frustrated at the lack of response he was getting, Daryl yelled at Josh, "She was pure and innocent, not like that Jezebel you're sleeping with. Is there going to be *another* unwed mother slipping out of town?"

Josh's head jerked around, and he pinned Daryl with a look that spoke of death—slow, painful death.

Daryl mistakingly took Josh's stillness for cowardice. In a drunken haze he raised his arms and encompassed the entire room. "That's where our illustrious sheriff was tonight. I heard Bill get her number from the operator."

The glass shattered in Josh's hand. Ice and soda mixed with his blood. He'd finally done it! he thought in a daze of physical pain and emotional anguish. He'd brought sweet, gentle Laura down to this level.

The jukebox skidded to a halt and not a sound emerged from anyone on the dance floor as Cal made his way across the room. "Daryl, if you possess even half the brains you were born with, shut up."

Daryl grabbed hold of the back of a chair to steady himself. He blinked his eyes and focused in on Josh sitting motionless on the stool. His stomach churned and he swayed when he saw the bloody hand, still in midair, and the stricken expression on Josh's face.

Cal pulled the stick out of Daryl's hand and yanked him across the room to the nearest exit.

Daryl's tears started to fall as he saw the pity and loathing directed his way from the dozen customers standing quietly and supportively behind Josh. "I didn't mean it, Josh." He wiped the back of his hand across his face. "Laura's a good girl, Josh." The echo of his last words carried across the room as the door closed behind him and Cal. "Just like my Joleen *used* to be."

Bill dashed around the bar with a clean white rag in his hand. He carefully lowered Josh's hand and looked at the cuts. One looked deep enough to require stitches, but the others appeared to be minor. "You need to go to the hospital, Josh."

Josh blinked. Daryl was gone. Cal was gone. And Laura was gone. Tender, loving Laura was now the talk of the bar because of him. He took the cloth from Bill and wrapped it around his hand. He didn't feel any pain from the cuts. The ache in his heart had numbed him.

Two male customers and Bill blocked the way as he headed for the door. "I don't think you should drive right now, Josh," Bill said. "One of us will take you to the hospital."

"Thanks, but I can manage on my own." Josh stepped around them and opened the door with his good hand.

Bill cleared his throat. "Josh?"

He stopped and turned halfway around.

"Daryl didn't mean it. He was drunk, or he would have never said that about Laura." When Josh just continued to stare, Bill added, "We all like Laura."

Josh nodded his head once and closed the door.

Dawn was slowly seeping through the lace curtains when Laura awoke to the feeling of someone watching her. Her eyes flew open, and she spotted Josh sitting at the bottom of the bed, staring at her. Alarmed, she noticed the white sling cradling his arm and sat up. "What happened?"

His jaw clenched as the sheet fell. "Cover yourself."

Laura blinked and glanced around the room. They were alone in the early morning dusk. She pulled the sheet up and tucked it around herself. "What happened to your arm?"

"My arm is fine. I just got half a dozen stitches in my hand." He had left the hospital over two hours before and had been sitting there watching her sleep ever since. She'd been curled up on her side, and every so often she would reach out as if looking for something. Or someone. Every time her small hand reached, it touched his heart.

"Can I get you something?" she asked.

"No, I came to return something." With great care he slowly opened his fist and dropped her keys onto the bed.

She glanced at her keys. "Why don't you come back to bed and try to get some sleep?"

Josh closed his eyes against the pain. He wanted nothing more than to climb back between those peach-colored sheets and hold her. He had tried, and failed. Some things in life you couldn't live down or forget. He said a prayer and six Hail Marys, even though he wasn't Catholic, that he hadn't totally destroyed Laura's reputation. His final act of love would be to leave her alone to get on with her life. Then people in town would pick up on some other topic soon enough.

He stood up and walked over to the window. He could make out the outline of Agnes's backyard. "I've been thinking."

Laura's gaze bore into his back. Something wasn't right. She was dying to know what had happened to his hand, but he obviously didn't want to talk about it. "Thinking about what?"

"Us."

That single word should have sent her into spirals of happiness, but something in his tone frightened her. "Oh."

He realized he couldn't turn around and face her. "I think it would be better for all concerned if we stop seeing each other."

Her heart seemed to stop beating. *So this was what it felt like to have your heart broken, she thought numbly.* She looked at his stiff back and wondered what she was supposed to say. Was she supposed to cry and beg him not to go? Pride kept her lips closed on the words she so desperately wanted to say.

Josh turned around at her silence. He'd expected tears and anger, not silence. Frustrated at her blank expression, he snapped, "Aren't you going to say anything?"

She gripped her hands together and willed her tears not to fall. "Why?"

He should have known she would ask the one question he didn't know how to answer. "It's for the best." He walked toward the door, and tears clouded his vision as he stepped over the belt he had bought her at the carnival. He still couldn't understand why a simple belt made her so happy, but he was glad he had bought it for her. He walked through the doorway and down the hall.

He stumbled as her final words reached him.

"May you find happiness on your path through life."

Laura waited until the sound of his car faded into the distance before allowing the tears to flow. She buried her face in her arms and cried. When she felt a ray of sunlight warm her cheek, she swiped at her tears and glared at the window. *Dawn had won again.*

In a burst of frustration she threw a pillow across the room and knocked the curtain down. Billowing white lace floated to the floor, crumbling like a melting phantom. She stared at the heap of lace and wiped her tears.

She was in love, and by hell, she was mad. Who in tarnation did Josh think he was to decide it was for the best if they stopped seeing each other? It wasn't for her best, and by the look on his face when he walked out, it wasn't for his either. Something had happened at Bronco Bill's, and she was going to find out what. There was no way she was allowing Josh to walk out of her life.

Joshua Franklin Langley was going to rue the day he had become the happiness on her path.

Ten

"'Lo," Josh mumbled.

"Thank God you're home," Agnes cried.

Josh squinted at the illuminated red digits on his clock. It was two-thirty in the morning. Where else would he be? He shifted the phone and yawned. "Who is this?"

"It's Agnes, you fool."

He let the name-calling slip by because he had called himself worst in the past twenty-four hours. "What's wrong?"

"Someone is prowling around Laura's house."

"*What?*" Josh yelled, coming instantly awake and jumping out of bed.

"I got up to get a glass of water, and you know how my kitchen window overlooks her yard?"

"Agnes!" He jammed his legs into a pair of jeans.

"Well, anyway, I saw this shape move across her yard. At first I thought I had imagined it, but then I stood very still and watched."

"What happened?" Josh snapped as he slid his foot into a sneaker.

"I saw it again. It walked by her windows and then around the front of her house. That's when I called you."

He pulled on the other sneaker. "Could it have been a dog or some other animal?"

"That big!" Josh heard her voice break. "No, it was a man, a big man." She hesitated, then said, "Or a bear."

Josh muttered a cross between a prayer and a curse. "Don't move, I'm on my way." He slammed down the phone, grabbed a shirt and his gun, and ran for the door. *Laura was in danger!*

He parked his car on the street behind Laura's and ran through the yards. His chest was heaving as he flattened himself against the rough exterior of her garage. Without making a sound, he worked his way to the front and studied the house. It looked quiet and sinister in the eerie moonlight. Glancing down at the revolver tucked into the waistband of his jeans, he wished he had remembered to put bullets in it before leaving his apartment.

He glanced up at Laura's dark bedroom windows and cursed. She was a beautiful woman living alone. The perfect victim. He crept farther into the shadows and tripped over a metal bucket. Regaining his balance, he held his breath as the loud *clang* died. He held perfectly still and watched the yard. Nothing moved.

Laura was jerked awake by a sound from outside. Probably a dog getting into the garbage cans, she thought. She threw back the covers and walked toward the window. She was about to yell at the animal when she noticed a man leaving the shadows of the garage and heading for the house.

Burglars! She reached for the phone and dialed Josh's number. On the fourth ring she heard his voice politely tell her that he couldn't come to the phone, but if she'd leave her name, number, and a short message he'd get back to her. Frustrated, angry, and scared, she snapped, "This is Laura Bryant. Where in the hell are you? Someone's about to break into my house, so if you find my blood-soaked body in the morning, it will be all your fault. Why in the hell am I talking to a machine? I hate damn machines."

She slammed the receiver down and yanked on a robe. Tying the belt, she realized she shouldn't have called Josh's home. She should have dialed 911. With trembling fingers she pushed the buttons and rapidly told a dispatcher what was going on. Help was on its way.

Feeling safer, she walked out into the hallway and slowly descended the stairs. She couldn't remember if she had locked the kitchen door. Partway down she saw a faint beam from a pocket flashlight at the living room window. She gripped the railing and whispered, "Chief, I hope to hell you're behind me. Better yet, get in front of me." The light moved away and shone on the next window. She held her breath until the light disappeared around the house.

She flew down the steps and ran for the back door. She was halfway across the kitchen when the knob turned and the door swung open. A quick glance proved the knives were too far; she'd never make it. Fear, desperation, and the will to live had her reaching for her only weapon. Hoisting the wooden chair, she let out a blood-curdling scream and hurled it with all her might.

Josh heard the scream and felt something connect with his head as the door slammed back into him, knocking him to the ground. He shook his head and tried to stand. He stilled as the snout of a forty-five was jammed into his face.

"Make my day."

Stunned, Josh focused on his deputy, Cal, who was standing with his legs spread and both hands on the butt of the powerful weapon. He had to be dreaming. Cal was dressed in red-and-white

striped pajamas and acting like Clint Eastwood.
This wasn't a dream, it was a nightmare!

Josh blinked as the back light was turned on,
flooding the yard in brilliance. "Put that gun
down, Cal, before someone gets hurt." As the
muzzle was lowered, he yelled, "Laura, are you all
right?"

Laura heard Josh's voice and pulled open the
door. She glanced down at Josh lying in the dirt, at
Cal dressed like a candy cane, and at Agnes flying
across the yard like an avenging angel in a long
white robe. "Did you get him?" Agnes asked.

"Who?" Laura asked.

"The burglar," Josh muttered.

"You mean the man who tripped over something
by my garage and then ran across the backyard to
the house?"

Embarrassed, Josh said, "That was me."

"You?" Laura said.

Confused, Cal clicked the safety back on his
gun. "You?" he muttered.

"But where's the burglar?" Agnes asked.

Laura felt Josh's heated gaze on her and pulled
the lapels of her robe together. "What burglar?"

"The one I called Josh about."

Laura glanced down at Josh, who was reclining
in a puddle from an earlier shower. "Aren't you
going to get up?"

He shifted his bandaged hand off the wet grass.
Heat was coiling in his stomach at the vision
Laura made standing there with her hair unruly
and wearing a satin peach robe that ended at
mid-thigh. Long, creamy legs stretched endlessly
above him. He'd been dreaming of those legs when
Agnes had called. He smiled, but lopsidedly. The
left side of his face felt numb. "What did you hit me
with?"

Horrified, Laura bent and studied his face.
"Where did it hit you?"

He raised his bandaged hand and touched the

lump that was forming on his head. "What was it?"

"Cal, help me get him inside so I can see better." With Cal on one side and Laura on the other, they carefully helped Josh stand and make his way into her kitchen.

Josh glanced down and stepped over a broken wooden chair. Damn, he thought, and here he was worried about her. The way she hurled chairs, a person would have to be nuts to break in. He allowed Laura to push him into one of the remaining chairs. When her gentle fingers ran through his hair and connected with the lump, he moaned with desire, not pain.

Laura heard his moan and went into action. Ice cubes were dumped into a dishtowel and placed gently over the lump.

Josh ground his teeth as the lapels of Laura's robe gaped farther apart. The sweet swelling of her breasts was at the perfect level for his gaze as she leaned over and held the ice pack. He clenched his fist and reminded himself why he had avoided Laura for the past twenty-four hours. He was trouble. The last thing he wanted for her was trouble.

"Cal, do you think he needs to have it x-rayed?" she asked.

Cal and Agnes moved in closer for a better look.

"I don't need my head x-rayed," Josh snapped. He already knew it was empty. "Cal, I want you to get the heavy-duty flashlight and look around the perimeter of Laura's house. See if you can find any footprints or signs of forced entry."

Laura glared and Agnes fretted as Josh placed the ice pack on the table and started a room-by-room search. The man was impossible! Laura fumed. He would rather walk around with a concussion than have her hands touch him. She should have clobbered him with the table instead.

By the time Josh announced the house was

secure, Cal had returned and reported that the only footprints in the soft soil were Josh's. There was no burglar. "Agnes, I think you must have been dreaming," Josh said.

The older woman bit a fingernail and shook her head. "No, I wasn't. There was something out there. I saw it."

Josh glanced at Cal, who shrugged and shook his head. "Will you be all right alone, Laura?"

"Of course."

Josh guided Agnes and Cal out the door. He hesitated on the threshold and looked back at Laura. His mouth opened to say something, then he snapped it closed. With slumped shoulders he started to pull the door shut. "Make sure it's locked this time," he said, then left.

Laura glanced up from her desk and forced her lips into a friendly smile as a man entered the newspaper office. Her head was pounding and her eyelids felt like sandpaper from lack of sleep. After everyone had cleared out the night before, she had paced, pouted, cried, and finally, in a fit of gloom, she had stuffed and roasted a chicken. Cooking was therapeutic. Usually.

"Hello," she said. "May I help you?"

The man in front of her desk shuffled his feet, straightened his tie, and flushed. "I'm Daryl Wiseman."

She smiled reassuringly at the nervous man. "My name is Laura Bryant. What can I do for you?"

"I know who you are, ma'am. That's why I came, to apologize to you."

Bewildered, Laura indicated he should sit down. "I see. What exactly are you apologizing for?"

Fifteen minutes later Laura escorted a beaming Daryl out of *The Union Station Review*'s office. She now knew what had happened at Bronco

Bill's. What she was going to do with the information she had no idea. She set the hands on the plastic clock dangling from the door, showing what time she'd be back, and locked up. A quick glance down Main Street, and she knew Josh had to be in his office. His car was parked outside. She walked over to where her bike was parked, threw her purse in the basket, and started home for lunch.

The window ledge bit into Josh's hand as he watched Laura ride down the street. He'd known the minute Daryl had walked into Laura's office. The mayor had phoned with that news. Then Harley had stopped in and reported that Daryl and Laura were sitting at her desk, drinking coffee. Josh had positioned himself to watch the plate-glass door of the newspaper office. When Daryl came out grinning, he knew Laura had forgiven Daryl. Josh wondered, as Laura pedaled out of sight, who was going to forgive him for giving up the best thing that had ever walked into his life.

He wearily rubbed a hand across his eyes and sighed. Lack of sleep was making him punchy. He should not have stayed up the rest of last night, sitting in his car in front of Laura's house. She had been perfectly safe, there hadn't been a prowler, and his head had sounded like a bass drum in a heavy metal band the entire time.

"Slow down, Gene, and repeat everything you just told me. This time slower." Josh covered the receiver with his hand and yawned. Squinting in the darkness, he read his clock. Midnight.

"Coyotes. I'm telling you, Josh, it was a coyote."

Josh glanced at the telephone and wondered if Gene had been out at Bronco Bill's. "Did you see them?"

"No, I heard them. Or, to be more precise, I heard *one*. I'm not sure how many there are."

Josh rubbed a hand down his face. "Gene, I've lived here all my life and never once have I seen or heard of a coyote being within a hundred miles of Union Station."

"Laugh if you want to, but I tell you there's one now. I was camping in the Sierras when I first heard one howl. Believe me, it's not a sound you're likely to forget. You break out in a sweat and chills shoot down your spine. It's eerie and haunting, and there's one in our town, Josh."

Josh sighed. Gene was a respectable citizen and never caused anyone trouble. "Okay, Gene, where did you hear this *coyote*?"

"Old man Peterson's place."

"Where?" Josh croaked.

"Right across the street from where I live, Josh."

Josh untangled himself from the sheets and jumped out of bed. "Are you sure?"

"If there wasn't a coyote standing in Laura's backyard two minutes ago, I'll eat my shorts."

Josh ran a hand through his hair and tried to think logically. Gene was a reasonable man, not known to fabricate stories. "Okay, Gene, I'm on my way. I want you to call Cal—and Sylas too. He's the best hunter in these parts. I'm going to stop at the office and pick up some rifles. We'll meet at your place in ten, fifteen minutes." He didn't wait for an answer as he slammed down the phone and moved.

Thirteen minutes later four men cautiously walked down Gene's driveway and headed for Laura's yard.

Laura woke and heard the distant murmuring of voices. What did a person have to do to get a decent night's sleep around here? she wondered irritably. Shrugging into her robe, she gazed out the front window. Beams from flashlights were bouncing around her yard, looking like a laser show. In a quick flash of light she recognized Cal. Her eyes narrowed as she studied the figure of another man. The pale bandage wrapped around his left hand confirmed her suspicions. Josh was in her yard again. For a man who said he didn't want to see her, he was turning up with amazing regularity.

A smile teased one corner of her mouth as she pulled on a pair of jeans and a top. She quickly ran a brush through her hair and stepped into a pair of shoes. Without making a sound she slid out the kitchen door and headed for the men.

She stumbled when she caught sight of the rifles they were carrying. Their backs were turned to her as they quietly argued among themselves. Hoping to appear calm, she walked to within a foot of them and asked, "What are we hunting tonight, boys?"

Four deadly rifles suddenly pointed at her.

"Christmas, Laura!" Cal roared. "Don't you know better than to sneak up on a person."

"Lord, missy, we could've pumped you full of holes," Gene said.

Josh's grip on his rifle relaxed as his blood once again started to flow. "What are you doing out here?" he snapped.

"I live here." Not liking his tone of voice, she turned her question to Cal. "What are you looking for tonight, Deputy?"

"Coyotes, ma'am."

Laura giggled. "In my backyard?"

Josh saw the situation slipping out of his control. "Gene reported hearing a coyote howling in your backyard. We came to investigate."

"I'm sorry, Gene, but I've been home all night." Pointing to her bedroom window on the second floor, she said, "I've been in bed for the past two hours with the windows open. Believe me, if a coyote howled in my backyard, I would have heard it."

Josh silently agreed with Laura, but he couldn't disregard what Gene had told him either. "Have any of you picked up any tracks or signs?"

When all three men answered no, Josh groaned. Great, he thought. First phantom prowlers, now disappearing coyotes. What in the hell was going on? "Laura, I want you to go back inside and lock the door. Try to go back to sleep." He turned to his men. "Let's spread out and cover a four-block radius. If we don't see any tracks or signs, we'll call it a night."

Laura turned and walked back to the house, muttering something about hoping there weren't any stray German shepherds out that night.

Josh sent his men in different directions and watched Laura close the door behind her. He mentally followed her through the kitchen, up the stairs, and into her bedroom. His body tightened with desire as he envisioned her undressing and climbing back in between cool sheets. Oh, hell, she could do worse than him. She didn't seem too upset by what Daryl had spouted in a drunken rage. She had forgiven him within fifteen minutes. Damn, she probably already knew about the false accusation Julie Burke had shouted at him twelve years before. He should have been the one to tell her the story. He at least owed her that.

With a sigh he flashed the beam of his light across Agnes's yard and slowly walked through the hedges, unaware of the lone figure watching from her bedroom window.

"Josh, you have to do something."

Josh looked at the woman sitting across from his desk, alternately biting her fingernails and wringing her hands. "Agnes, what would you like me to do?"

"Move her out of that house."

He closed his eyes and sighed. Why did everyone expect him to do something? It wasn't his house. He hadn't once witnessed the strange goings-on at Laura's house, and, dammit, he had spent more time there than she had this past week. He had come to the conclusion at three o'clock in the morning, sitting in his car in front of her house, that Laura wasn't crazy. The house wasn't even possessed by sinister spirits. It was the town! The whole blasted town had gone stark raving bonkers.

In the past week he had locked up Ernest, the town's undertaker, for sprinkling holy water around the outside of Laura's house. He had hauled in the entire women's auxiliary for nailing heads of garlic above Laura's windows and doors, and released them only when Laura refused to press charges. To top it off, he had awakened Laura at two o'clock in the morning to tell her a neighbor was complaining that she was playing her drums too loudly.

The police dispatcher was plagued with complaints ranging from strange noises to offensive odors. Laura had been invited to be a guest in more houses than the president. Even Kelli was talking about calling in a priest for an exorcism. Everyone, from the local mechanic to the mayor, was convinced that old man Peterson was out to harm Laura.

The only one who seemed totally unconcerned was Laura. After the third night of having her sleep interrupted, she had calmly walked into the police station and dropped off a spare key to her house. She'd smiled pleasantly and asked that he or Cal lock up on their way out from investigating whatever the town dreamed up next.

"Josh? Josh, are you listening to me?" Agnes

asked. "I heard those stories about Mr. Peterson, but never believed them. Albert was a lonely old man who loved his dog. He didn't deserve those frightful stories. Now I'm not too sure."

"What else have you seen?"

"It's not that I've seen anything. I feel it."

"Feel what?" Josh asked.

"The house." At Josh's raised brows, she said, "It watches me."

Josh's temper snapped, and he slammed his fist down on the desk. "You expect me to drag a perfectly normal woman from her home because the house *watches you!*" He shoved back his chair and stood. "Listen, Agnes, there are no such things as ghosts. Laura's the one who has been living and sleeping in that house, and she says she hasn't seen or heard anything out of the ordinary. I'm beginning to believe she and I are the last sane people in this town."

Tears pooled in Agnes's eyes. "You don't care what happens to her."

Josh's shoulders sagged in defeat. Sighing with exhaustion, he walked over to the window and stared down the street toward the newspaper office. "Yes, I do." He rested his forehead against the cool pane of glass. "More than you'll ever know, Agnes. More than you'll ever know."

Eleven

Laura studied the stubborn expression on Ed's face and wondered why Agnes had lovingly nick-named him "dumpling." His two sons, Nicolai and Mikhail, were just as large as he, but somewhere along the line they must have picked up some of their mother's finer qualities. They were smiling. "Ed, Nicolai, and Mikhail," she said pleasantly, "I really appreciate the thought, but I don't think it's necessary."

Ed lowered his sleeping bag and a bag of grocer-ies to the kitchen table. "Agnes says you won't stay with her."

Was this how Alice felt when she ate the mush-room and got smaller and smaller? Laura won-dered, staring at the three men surrounding her. How in the world had she managed to shrink in her own kitchen? "Ed, I live here. Why should I stay with her?"

"Spooks, *da*?"

"No, Ed, there are no ghosts."

Mikhail, who at eighteen was as tall as his father, lowered another bag of groceries to the table. "Agnes told us that old man Peterson is trying to drive you from his house."

"It's my house, or, I should say, it's the bank's and mine. There hasn't been any sign of Mr. Peterson."

Nicolai glanced around in morbid fascination, as only a sixteen-year-old would. "The whole town's talking about how old man Peterson wants you out." A look of disappointment showed on his youthful face when nothing popped out of the woodwork or slithered across the floor.

Laura sighed in defeat when Ed walked into her living room and started to unroll his sleeping bag. Still hoping to discourage them, though, she said, "You will have to sleep on the floor. I don't have a spare bed or even a couch." When the boys joined their father and unrolled their bags, she desperately added, "I don't even have a television."

"That be good," Ed said in a voice that rumbled. "My sons read tonight. Mikhail goes to university soon. He be great doctor one day." Ed slowly shook his head as he gazed at his younger son. "Nicolai needs much help with school. They tell me he is average. I didn't leave Russia for my son to be this average. I came to America for my sons to be great."

Laura smiled sympathetically at Nicolai. "There's no shame in being average. There's only shame in not trying."

Nicolai smiled his thanks. Ed grunted, and Mikhail headed for the kitchen to dig through the grocery bags.

By eleven Laura could barely pull herself up the stairs to her bedroom. Her Russian sentries had been fascinated with everything she knew about American Indians. When they found out she was part Navaho, they sat wide-eyed and devoured every word she spoke. She repeated stories, legends, and facts from memory as they ate through a bag and a half of groceries. She finally pleaded fatigue, and with a promise that she would find some pictures of Indians in the morning for them, they had let her go upstairs.

She turned off her bedroom light and settled under the covers. Now maybe, with three huge bodyguards sleeping in her living room, the town and the police department would let her get one full night's sleep. She wondered if Josh knew about the slumber party she was throwing in her living room.

The only good thing coming from these alleged hauntings, she mused, was that she was seeing Josh at least once a day. She knew and understood why he had backed off, and it made her love him more. He had loved her enough to push her away before she got hurt. A secret smile curved her mouth as she nestled deeper into the pillow. She wondered what he would do when he realized she didn't give a tinker's damn what the town said. The smile stayed on her lips as she slipped into sleep.

Josh glanced at the clock on his dash as Laura's bedroom light flicked off. Eleven o'clock. He stretched his legs into a more comfortable position, then reached for his Thermos and poured himself a cup of steaming coffee. It looked like another long night. He raised the cup and whispered, "Pleasant dreams, love."

Nicolai woke and glanced around the dark room. Yawning, he pushed back his sleeping bag and headed for the stairs, and the bathroom. In his muddled state, he made the mistake of a lifetime. He reached for the first door on the left, Laura's bedroom, instead of the door on the right.

In the dimly lit hall, a massive Indian materialized, blocking Laura's bedroom door. Nicolai's eyes bulged as the Indian waved a writhing rattlesnake under his nose. Terrified, he threw up his arms and screamed. His scream was still echoing off walls and ceilings, amplifying as it traveled down the stairs, when he turned and fled into an empty bedroom. He slammed the door and turned the pitiful lock that would never stop the furious warrior from taking his scalp. Racing across the room, he threw open the window. His terrified screams, mixed with English and Russian pleas for help and for his father, filled the air and floated across the neighborhood.

Laura fell out of bed and connected with the hardwood floor when someone, or something, yelled outside her bedroom door. The sound turned her blood cold, and for one horrifying moment she was paralyzed with fear. She lay there stunned until she heard Nicolai's pleas for help in the next room. Scrambling to her feet, she ran for the door.

Josh spilled a half-cup of coffee down the front of his shirt when the unearthly scream surrounded the police cruiser. He flew from the car, pulled his gun, and sprinted toward Laura's house. Sobbing cries for help filled the air. With shaking fingers he jammed the spare key into the door, realizing only then that it wasn't Laura screaming.

Ed and Mikhail rolled over and collided with each other as Nicolai's screams shook the house. With curses and grunts they stumbled around in the dark trying to find the light switch. Ed tripped over his son's empty sleeping bag, lost his balance, and landed rearfirst on top of one of Laura's barrel cactuses. His painful bellows filled the living room.

Laura stumbled out into the hall and groped for the light switch. Nothing. What in the world had happened to the lights? She felt her way down to the room where Nicolai was still screaming. Her fists pounded on the locked door. "Nicolai, let me in. It's Laura." When Ed's excruciating cry split the air, she dropped her fist and flattened herself against the wall. Oh, sweet mother, what was happening?

Josh ignored whoever was howling in the living room and dashed up the stairs. His first concern was Laura. He stumbled, whacked his knee on the steps, and cursed the darkness. Where in the hell were the lights?

Gene silently disengaged the safety on his rifle and crept through the kitchen door that Josh had left open. Sucking in a deep breath, he prayed he could remember exactly how Chuck Norris did this. Sweat broke out across his forehead at the sounds of someone being murdered in the living room. Exhaling, he dive-rolled into the room, heading for his first heroic deed.

Rambo would have been proud of the dive. It was the roll that screwed things up. Nowhere in any of those movies did they explain what would happen if you were out of shape and had a beer belly hanging six inches over your belt. Gene dove, did a half-roll, fell sideways like a beached whale, and shot Laura's kitchen light.

Nicolai heard the shot, ripped through the screen, and climbed onto the sagging porch roof. He wildly flapped his arms and shouted as a fire truck pulled up into the driveway.

Mikhail abandoned any hope of rescuing his father from whatever beast was attacking him and threw open the living room door. Flashing red lights, sirens, and curious neighbors were surrounding the house as he hurried onto the porch. He took two steps, heard the distinct splintering of wood, and fell through the rotted porch floor. When something scurried across the top of his bare foot, he started to yell for help and forgiveness. Neighbors came running, and were more astonished at the deeds he was confessing to than by his being half swallowed by the porch.

Laura's heart stopped at the sound of the shot. It

had come from inside the house. She squeezed herself into the farthest corner of the hall and prayed she would become invisible. Where was Josh? she wondered frantically. He had practically lived there all week, and now, when she desperately needed him, he was nowhere around. She wished to God he were there.

Or was that Josh shooting? Or was Josh being shot at?

Scratch that earlier wish, God, she prayed. Don't let Josh be anywhere near here. Send him far, far away.

In a pitifully low whisper, she said, "Chief? Chief, where are you?" She didn't feel the sense of security that usually surrounded her when the chief was near. "I'm sorry I yelled at you before. You can come out of hiding."

Nothing.

"If you want to terrorize the town, that's fine by me, if only you make sure Josh is unhurt." Tears blurred her vision, and she felt suddenly all alone in the world. "Please, Chief Snuggle Bear. I know you're supposed to be my guardian spirit, but Josh is my life. Don't you understand, without him I'm not alive!"

Josh felt the hair on the back of his neck rise when a shot was fired downstairs. He stood on the landing, torn between finding Laura and seeing what was going on down there. He followed his heart. In three strides he was through her open bedroom door and headed for the bed. He searched the sheets, came up with one pillow, but no Laura. She was gone!

He hurried back into the darkened hall, frantically calling her name. "Laura! Laura, where are you?"

Laura pushed away from the wall and hurled herself in the direction of his voice. "Josh!"

He turned and stumbled as her body locked with

his. The gun fell from his hand as he pulled her close and kissed her. She was safe and in his arms. He would never let her go again.

Laura heard the sounds of sirens, of people yelling and running in a hundred different directions. She deepened the kiss and encircled his neck with loving hands. If the ghost of old man Peterson walked up to them right that minute, she'd probably kiss him too. She was right where she wanted to be, in Josh's arms, and she was never letting him go.

Josh broke the kiss long enough to answer Cal, who was anxiously calling his name from the kitchen. "Who did the shooting, Cal?" he yelled back.

A beam of light encircled the couple embracing at the top of the stairs. "Gene."

"Who did he hit?"

"We don't know what he was aiming for, but he killed Laura's kitchen light."

Laura chuckled and snuggled closer to Josh. "Was that the extent of the damage?" Josh asked.

"Ed sat on one of her cactuses and pretty well smashed it. Mikhail fell through the front porch, and the fire department is getting Nicolai off the porch roof now."

Laura looked down and squinted into the light. "No one was hurt?"

"No, ma'am."

"Good. Clear the house, Cal, and lock the door behind you." She reached up and captured Josh's chuckle with her lips.

Cal lowered the light and cleared his throat. He discreetly waited another moment before yelling up the stairs, "Josh, Laura, the women's auxiliary wants to plug in their coffeepot, but you seem to have blown a fuse."

Josh and Laura groaned in defeat. "The fuse box is in the pantry, Cal," Laura told him. "You'll find extra fuses right next to it." She figured they still had two minutes of total privacy, and she wasn't going to waste a second of it. She reached up and ran her tongue over Josh's lower lip.

Laura raised her head from its pillow, Josh's chest, and frowned as dawn lightened the room. She looked down at Josh and asked, "You aren't leaving, are you?"

He ran his hand up her thigh. "Are you throwing me out?"

She captured his hand and brought it to her lips. Her tongue was gentle as it traced the recent crescent-shaped scar on his palm. "Never. I want you to stay, always." She rolled off him and dragged the sheet up over her breasts. "I know why you left before. I love you, Josh. It doesn't matter what anyone says about you, or me, as long as we're together."

He ran a finger down her cheek and lifted her chin up so he could read her eyes. "I should have told you about Julie before, but it isn't one of the highlights of my life. Half the time I'm still not sure if I've outlived the bad name."

"Josh, you outlived the name hellion a long time ago. The people in this town love and respect you." She smiled at his skeptical look. "Why do you think they have been going crazy thinking of new ways to throw us together?"

"They've been behind the ghosts, coyotes, and prowlers?"

"Afraid so."

"You knew the whole time."

"No. I didn't catch on until the night with the coyotes."

Josh thought back to that night. "What gave it away?"

"Cal whispered in my ear that the next time I

come outside in the middle of the night, to wear something more seductive than jeans." She smoothed her thumb over his lower lip. "He said the peach-colored robe had had a very healthy effect on you."

Josh cupped her hip and pulled her closer. "Did he now?"

"Umm-hmm."

"I think I'll give that man a raise." He bent and kissed her parted lips. "Was tonight staged?"

"No. I'm sure they had something planned, but Nicolai spoiled it."

Josh kissed her throat, then trailed his lips across her shoulder. "You really should be ashamed of yourself, telling Indian war stories to a sixteen-year-old kid. Especially when he was staying in a haunted house. No wonder he thought he saw an Indian waving a rattlesnake." Josh's mouth slid lower and nipped at a pouting nipple. "You still haven't answered my question."

She arched her back and brought the peak back to his lips. "What question was that?"

He raised his head. Their gazes locked. "If I have to lock up another football player for disorderly conduct, I might not have a job come next election. But I promise you, you will never question my love for you."

"I heard about how you single-handedly lost the state championship for the Tigers, and I love you for it. What you did was right. I shouldn't tell you this, but the mayor is concerned about Tom. It seems he likes to hit the frat parties at college more than his books. I overheard him tell Gene that he wished there were a stronger police department on the campus."

Josh chuckled. "I'll be damned."

"Not yet you're not, but I hear the basketball team has a good shot at the title this year, so behave yourself."

He placed a quick kiss in the valley between her breasts. "Are you going to keep me out of trouble by marrying me?"

A slow, seductive smile curved her lips as she pulled him closer. "Try getting out of it."

Laura cautiously slipped out from under Josh's arm. Pulling on a robe, she quietly left the room. Without making a sound and avoiding the steps that creaked, she hurried to the third floor.

Sadness engulfed her as she opened the door to the chief's room. It was empty except for the steamer trunk pushed back into a far corner. No baskets littered the floor, no bows and arrows adorned the walls. Even her stuffed bear was gone.

She walked over to the trunk and lovingly caressed the brass fittings. The chief was gone. Two lone tears slid down her cheek. "Good-bye, Chief." She bit her lower lip. "I didn't even get a chance to thank you. You knew Josh was the one, didn't you? Is that why you left? Is your job over now that Josh is here for me?" She looked around the room and wiped at the tears.

The chief wasn't going to answer her. He never did. She already knew the answer. It was in her heart. She pressed a kiss to the tips of her fingers and blew it into the sunlight streaming in through the window. "Good-bye, Chief Snuggle Bear. Wherever you travel, go with a piece of my heart."

Laura felt a sense of security and love engulf her as she closed the door and started down the stairs. A brilliant smile lit her face as she headed for Josh and their future.

Epilogue

One year later . . .

Laura's fingers stilled on the keyboard. Was that a noise from Sara's room? She saved the article she was in the middle of writing and turned off the computer. Josh had bought her the electronic marvel the day she told him he was going to become a father. She would continue to write for *The Union Station Review*, but now most of it could be done at home.

She slowly got to her feet and headed for the stairs and Sara's room. Saturday Sara Ann Langley would be celebrating her first month's birthday. Her father was arranging a barbecue in honor of such a prestigious event. Laura walked down the hall, past her and Josh's bedroom, and entered the brightly papered nursery.

Rainbows clung to the walls, shelves overflowed with assorted stuffed animals, and dazzling yellow curtains hung at the windows. Not hearing a sound from her daughter, Laura tiptoed over to the crib. Dark hair, like her father's, covered her sweet head, and tiny lips greedily sucked on a tiny pink thumb. Laura watched her tiny back rise and fall in an even rhythm.

Satisfied Sara was fine, she turned to go start lunch for Josh, when a look of shock crossed her face. Nestled at the bottom of the crib was her old childhood companion, Snuggle Bear.

Laura flew from the room and up to the third floor. Her hands were sweating and shaking as she opened the door she had closed one year before. Sunlight flooded the room. Baskets were lined up under the window, bows were artfully displayed on the walls, along with assorted arrows. The empty trunk was open and sitting in the middle of the room. Laura's knees gave out as she plopped down on the folded red blanket. The chief was back!

He hadn't come back for her. He had come to watch over Sara! Her four-week-old daughter had acquired a *guardian spirit*! What in the world was she going to tell Josh?

As if her thoughts had conjured him up, Laura heard him softly call her name. He was home early for lunch. A strangled cry was the best she could muster in answer to his persistent call.

Josh climbed the stairs to the third floor and headed for the open door. What was Laura doing up there? he wondered. No one ever went up there. He smiled at his wife's guilty expression and glanced around. His interest was kindled as he walked over and reverently touched an ancient bow. These weren't the kinds of bows a tourist could buy in a souvenir shop. These were the real McCoys.

He noticed his wife's pallor and knelt down in front of her. He hoped she hadn't hurt herself moving the trunk. She was stubborn and opinionated, and he loved her dearly. Trying for a light note, he said, "So these are the family heirlooms?"

Laura felt a hysterical bubble of laughter rise up in her throat and quickly squashed it. This was not the time or place for hysterics. She must be calm and level-headed when she explained this one to Josh. Her voice held a slight quiver as she said, "Josh, there is one other heirloom . . ."

THE EDITOR'S CORNER

It's going to be a merry month, indeed, for all of us LOVESWEPT devotees with romances that are charming, delightful, moving, and hot!

First, one of Deborah Smith's most romantic, dreamy love stories ever, CAMELOT, LOVESWEPT #468. Deb sweeps you away to sultry Florida, a setting guaranteed to inspire as much fantasizing in you as it does in heroine Agnes Hamilton. The story opens on a stormy night when Agnes has been thinking and dreaming about the love story recorded in the diary of a knight of Britain's Middle Ages. He seems almost real to her. When the horses on her breeding farm need her help to shelter from the wind and rain, Agnes forges out into the night—only to meet a man on horseback who seems for all the world like her knight of old. Who is the wickedly handsome John Bartholomew and dare she trust their instant attraction to each other? This is a LOVESWEPT to read slowly so you can enjoy each delicious phrase of a beautiful, sensual, exciting story.

Welcome a marvelous new talent to our fold, Virginia Leigh, whose SECRET KEEPER, LOVESWEPT #469, is her first published novel. Heroine Mallory Bennett is beautiful, sexy—and looking her worst in mud-spattered jeans (sounds like real life, huh?), when hero Jake Gallegher spots her in the lobby of his restaurant. From the first he knows she's Trouble . . . and he senses a deep mystery about her. Intrigued, he sets out to probe her secrets and find the way to her heart. Don't miss this moving and thrilling love story by one of our New Faces of '91!

Joan Elliott Pickart is back with a funny, tender, sizzler MEMORIES, LOVESWEPT #470. This is an irresistible story of a second chance at love for Minty Westerly and Chism Talbert. Minty grew up happy and privileged

Chism grew up troubled and the caretaker's son. But status and money couldn't come between them for they had all the optimism of the young in love. Then Chism broke Minty's heart, disappearing on the same night they were to elope. Now, back in town, no longer an angry young man, but still full of passion, Chism encounters Minty, a woman made cautious by his betrayal. Their reunion is explosive—full of pain and undimmed passion . . . and real love. You'll revel in the steps this marvelous couple takes along the path to true love!

That marvelous romantic Linda Cajio gives you her best in EARTH ANGEL, LOVESWEPT #471, next month. Heroine Catherine Wagner is a lady with a lot on her mind—rescuing her family business from a ruthless and greedy relative while pursuing the cause of her life. When she meets charismatic banker Miles Kitteridge she thinks he must be too good to be true. His touch, his fleeting kisses leave her weak-kneed. But is he on to her game? And, if so, can she trust him? Miles knows he wants the passionate rebel in his arms forever . . . but capturing her may be the toughest job of his life! A real winner from Linda!

Welcome another one of our fabulous New Faces of '91, Theresa Gladden, with her utterly charming debut novel, ROMANCING SUSAN, LOVESWEPT #472. First, devastatingly handsome Matt Martinelli steals Susan Wright's parking space—then he seems determined to steal her heart! And Susan fears she's just going to be a pushover for his knock-'em-dead grin and gypsy eyes. She resists his lures . . . but when he gains an ally in her matchmaking great aunt, Susan's in trouble—delightfully so. A love story of soft Southern nights and sweet romancing that you'll long remember!

Patt Bucheister strikes again with one of her best ever sensual charmers, HOT PURSUIT, LOVESWEPT #473. Rugged he-man Denver Sierra is every woman's dream and a man who will not take no for an answer. Lucky Courtney Caine! But it takes her a while to realize just how lucky she is. Courtney has hidden in the peaceful shadows cast by her performing family. Denver is determined to draw her out into the bright sunshine of life . . . and to melt her icy fears with the warmth of his affection and the fire of his desire. Bravo, Patt!

We trust that as always you'll find just the romances you want in all six of our LOVESWEPTs next month. Don't forget our new imprint, FANFARE, if you want more of the very best in women's popular fiction. On sale next month from FANFARE are three marvelous novels that we guarantee will keep you riveted. MORTAL SINS is a mesmerizing contemporary novel of family secrets, love and unforgettable intrigue from a dynamic writing duo Dianne Edouard and Sandra Ware. THE SCHEMERS by Lois Wolfe is a rich, thrilling historical novel set during the Civil War with the most unlikely—and marvelous—heroine and hero. She's a British aristocrat, he's a half Apache army scout. Be sure also to put Joan Dial's sweeping historical FROM A FAR COUNTRY on your list of must-buy fiction. This enthralling novel will take you on a romantic journey between continents . . . and the hearts and souls of its unforgettable characters.

Ah, so much for you to look forward to in the merry month ahead.

Warm good wishes,

Carolyn Nichols

Carolyn Nichols
Editor
LOVESWEPT
Bantam Books
666 Fifth Avenue
New York, NY 10102-0023

THE LATEST IN BOOKS AND AUDIO CASSETTES

Paperbacks

☐	28671	**NOBODY'S FAULT** Nancy Holmes	$5.95
☐	28412	**A SEASON OF SWANS** Celeste De Blasis	$5.95
☐	28354	**SEDUCTION** Amanda Quick	$4.50
☐	28594	**SURRENDER** Amanda Quick	$4.50
☐	28435	**WORLD OF DIFFERENCE** Leonia Blair	$5.95
☐	28416	**RIGHTFULLY MINE** Doris Mortman	$5.95
☐	27032	**FIRST BORN** Doris Mortman	$4.95
☐	27283	**BRAZEN VIRTUE** Nora Roberts	$4.50
☐	27891	**PEOPLE LIKE US** Dominick Dunne	$4.95
☐	27260	**WILD SWAN** Celeste De Blasis	$5.95
☐	25692	**SWAN'S CHANCE** Celeste De Blasis	$5.95
☐	27790	**A WOMAN OF SUBSTANCE** Barbara Taylor Bradford	$5.95

Audio

☐	**SEPTEMBER** by Rosamunde Pilcher Performance by Lynn Redgrave 180 Mins. Double Cassette	45241-X	$15.95
☐	**THE SHELL SEEKERS** by Rosamunde Pilcher Performance by Lynn Redgrave 180 Mins. Double Cassette	48183-9	$14.95
☐	**COLD SASSY TREE** by Olive Ann Burns Performance by Richard Thomas 180 Mins. Double Cassette	45166-9	$14.95
☐	**NOBODY'S FAULT** by Nancy Holmes Performance by Geraldine James 180 Mins. Double Cassette	45250-9	$14.95

60 Minutes to a Better, More Beautiful You!

Now it's easier than ever to awaken your sensuality, stay slim forever—even make yourself irresistible. With Bantam's bestselling subliminal audio tapes, you're only 60 minutes away from a better, more beautiful you!

__ 45004-2	**Slim Forever**	$8.95
__ 45035-2	**Stop Smoking Forever**	$8.95
__ 45022-0	**Positively Change Your Life**	$8.95
__ 45041-7	**Stress Free Forever**	$8.95
__ 45106-5	**Get a Good Night's Sleep**	$7.95
__ 45094-8	**Improve Your Concentration**	$7.95
__ 45172-3	**Develop A Perfect Memory**	$8.95

Bantam Books, Dept. LT, 414 East Golf Road, Des Plaines, IL 60016

Please send me the items I have checked above. I am enclosing $ _____ (please add $2.50 to cover postage and handling). Send check or money order, no cash or C.O.D.s please. (Tape offer good in USA only.)

Mr/Ms _____

Address _____

City/State _____ Zip _____

LT-2/91

Please allow four to six weeks for delivery.
Prices and availability subject to change without notice.

NEW!

Handsome Book Covers Specially Designed To Fit Loveswept Books

Our new French Calf Vinyl book covers come in a set of three great colors— royal blue, scarlet red and kachina green.

Each 7" × 9½" book cover has two deep vertical pockets, a handy sewn-in bookmark, and is soil and scratch resistant.

To order your set, use the form below.